Élisée Reclus, John Lillie, Bertha Ness

The History of a Mountain

Élisée Reclus, John Lillie, Bertha Ness

The History of a Mountain

ISBN/EAN: 9783337287252

Printed in Europe, USA, Canada, Australia, Japan

Cover: Foto ©Andreas Hilbeck / pixelio.de

More available books at **www.hansebooks.com**

THE HISTORY

OF

A MOUNTAIN

BY

ELISÉE RECLUS

ILLUSTRATED BY L. BENNETT

THE HISTORY OF A MOUNTAIN

By ELISÉE RECLUS

Translated from the French

By BERTHA NESS AND JOHN LILLIE

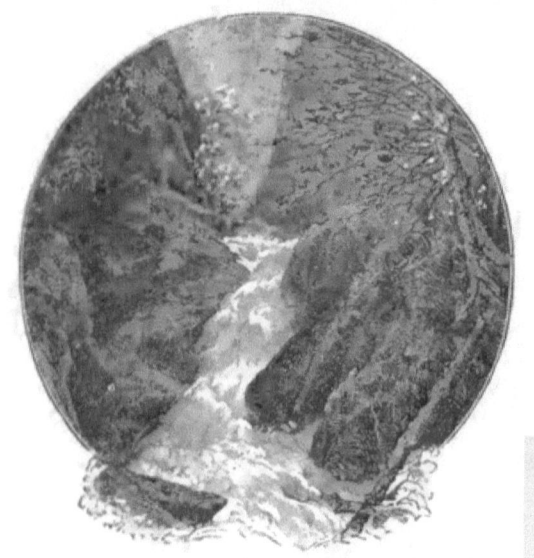

ILLUSTRATED BY L. BENNETT

NEW YORK
HARPER & BROTHERS, FRANKLIN SQUARE
1881

CONTENTS.

LIST OF ILLUSTRATIONS.

THE HISTORY

OF

A MOUNTAIN.

CHAPTER I.

THE RETREAT.

I was sad, downcast, weary of my life. Fate had
dealt hardly with me; it had robbed me of all who were
dear to me, had ruined my plans, frustrated all my hopes.
People whom I called my friends had turned against me
when they beheld me assailed by misfortune; all mankind, with its conflicting interests and its unrestrained
passions, appeared repulsive in my eyes. Cost what it

1*

might, I was determined to run away, either to die, or in solitude to regain my vigor and peace of mind.

Without knowing exactly whither my steps were leading me, I turned towards those great mountains whose jagged crests I beheld breaking the distant line of the horizon.

On I went, following by-paths, and in the evening stopping before isolated inns. The sound of a human voice, the noise of a footstep, made me shudder; but when I was walking alone I listened with melancholy pleasure to the birds singing, the river murmuring, and the thousand strains proceeding from the vast woods.

Walking, as chance led me, either along the high-road or footpath, at last I reached the first defile of the mountain. The wide plain, scored with indentations, stopped abruptly at the foot of the rocks and slopes shaded by chestnut-trees. The lofty blue peaks, seen from afar, had disappeared behind other crests, which were not so high, yet nearer to me. By my side the river, which, lower down, falling over boulders, extended into a vast sheet of water, flowed rapidly down between the shining rocks, clad with a blackish-hued moss. Above each bank a low hill, the first lesser chain of the mountains, reared up its escarpments and bore upon its summit the ruins of a large tower, formerly the warder of the valley. I felt shut in between two walls; I had quitted the region of large towns, of smoke and hubbub; enemies and false friends were left behind.

It was the first time for very long that I had felt a sensation of real gladness. My step became brisker, my glance more confident; I stood still that I might enjoy

"THIS WAS THE LAST HABITATION."

the delight of inhaling the pure air coming down from the monntain.

There are no more stone, dust, or mud covered high-roads in this country: now I have left the low-lying plains; I am in the mountain, which no hand has yet subdned! A foot-track formed by goats and goatherds turns aside from the broader road, which follows the bottom of the valley, and ascends obliquely along the hill-side. This is the road which I take, so that I may be quite sure of at last being alone. Every step bringing me higher, I notice how the people walking along the path beneath gradnally grow smaller and smaller. The hamlets and villages are half hidden from my sight by their own smoke, a bluish-gray mist which creeps slowly over the heights, and on its way leaves fragments of itself clinging to the outskirts of the forest.

Towards evening, after having made the circuit of several rocky declivities, having passed over numerous ravines, and crossed many brawling streamlets by jumping from stone to stone, I reached the base of a height rising far above rocks, woods, and pastnres. At the top a smoky cabin, and sheep grazing on the slopes around, appeared in sight. This yellowish path wonnd upwards to the cabin like a piece of unrolled ribbon, and there seemed to stop. Farther on, I could discern nothing but great stony ravines, landslips, waterfalls, snow, and glaciers. This was the last habitation of man. It was the cabin which for long months shonld serve as my place of refuge. A dog, then a shepherd, received me as if they were friends.

Henceforward, being free, I allowed nature slowly to renew my life. At times I would wander in the midst of a chaos of stones, which had been hurled down from a rocky ridge; at others I would walk as chance led me in a forest of pine-trees; then, again, I would climb to the upper crests, and seat myself upon some peak overlooking the whole scene; often I would plunge into a deep, black ravine, in which I could imagine that I had fled into the bowels of the earth.

Gradually, under the influence of time and nature, the lugubrious phantoms which haunted my memory relaxed their hold. I no longer walked merely to escape from my recollections, but also to allow myself to be imbued with the impressions of all around me, and to enjoy them as if unconsciously.

If ever, since having set my foot upon the mountain, I had experienced a sensation of gladness, it was owing to the fact of my having entered into solitude, and that rocks, forests, a whole new world, had risen up between me and the past; yet one fine day I understood that a new passion had crept into my soul. I loved the mountain for its own sake. I loved its superb calm face, lighted up by the sun while we were still left in gloom; I loved its mighty shoulders, laden with ice full of blue reflections; its sides, whereon pastures alternated with forests and waste ground; its huge roots stretched out afar like those of an enormous tree, separated by valleys, with their respective rivulets, cascades, lakes, and meadows; I loved everything belonging to the mountain, down to the yellow or green moss growing upon the rocks, down to the stone gleaming in the midst of the turf.

Just in the same manner the shepherd, who, as a representative of that humankind from which I was escap-

ing, at first almost displeased me, had gradually become
necessary to me; I felt my confidence in and friendship
for him awaken. I no longer confined myself to thank-
ing him for the food which he brought and the services
which he rendered me. But I studied him; I tried to
learn all that he could teach me. Very slender were
his appliances for instruction; but when once the love
of nature had taken possession of me, it was he who
taught me to know the mountain on which the flocks
grazed and at whose base he was born. He told me
the names of the plants, showed me the rocks in which
crystals and rare stones were to be found, accompanied
me to the edges of dizzy whirlpools to point out the line
I must pursue where it was difficult to cross. From the
top of the peaks he indicated the valleys, traced out the
course of the torrents; then, having returned to our
smoky cabin, related to me the history of the country
and its local legends.

In exchange, I explained many things to him which
he did not, and had never even desired to, understand.
But his intelligence expanded by degrees; it became rapacious. When I saw his eye brighten and his lips
smile, I took delight in repeating to him the little that I
knew. Intellect dawned upon that face, until lately so
dull and heavy. From being as careless as he had hitherto been, he was metamorphosed into a man capable of
reflecting both on himself and the objects surrounding
him.

And, while teaching my companion, I taught myself;
for, in trying to explain nature's phenomena to the shepherd, I ended in understanding them better, and became
my own pupil.

Thus incited by the double interest which the love of nature and sympathy with my companion imparted to me, I endeavored to become acquainted both with the present life and past history of the mountain upon which we dwelt like parasites upon an elephant's hide. I studied the enormous mass, in the rocks of which it is formed; in the irregularities of the ground which, according to the different points of view, the hours and the seasons imparted to it—such great diversity of aspects, so lovely or so terrible. I studied it in its snow, its ice, and the weather that assailed it; in the plants and animals inhabiting its surface.

I also strove to understand what influence the mountain had had upon the poetry and history of nations, the part it had played in the movements of the different peoples and in the progress of all mankind.

That which I did learn I owe to the co-operation of my shepherd, and also, since I ought to tell everything,

to that of the creeping insects, of the butterflies and birds of song.

Had I not spent long hours lying on the grass, watching or listening to those tiny beings, my brothers, perhaps I should not so well have understood how alive is also that vast earth which bears in its bosom all those infinitely small creatures, and carries them away with us into unfathomable space.

Chapter II.

PEAKS AND VALLEYS.

Seen from the plain, the mountain is of a very simple form; it is a small, jagged cone, rising, amid other points of unequal height, upon a blue wall streaked with pink and white, which bounds one entire side of the horizon. It was as if I were looking from afar at a monster saw with unevenly cut teeth; one of these teeth is the mountain upon which wandered my feet.

Nevertheless, the small cone which I distinguished from its inferior companions, a simple grain of sand upon that grain of sand which is the earth, now appeared to me like a world. From my hut I can easily see, a few hundred yards above my head, a ridge of rock which seems to be the summit, yet no sooner do I climb up to it than another peak rises up beyond the snow. I gain a second terrace, and the mountain appears again to change its form. From every point, every ravine, every declivity, the landscape is displayed under a fresh aspect, under another form. Taken by itself, the mountain is a whole group of mountains, just as in the midst of the sea each billow is built up of innumerable tiny wavelets. To understand the architecture of the whole mountain, it must be studied, be surveyed in every direction; every elevation should be ascended, every gorge penetrated. Like everything else, it is inexhaustible for all who wish to know it in its entirety.

The height upon which I best loved to sit was not the crowning elevation where I might place myself like a king upon a throne, thence to contemplate the kingdoms extended at his feet. I felt happier upon the next lower summit, whence my glance could at the same time descend to the lowest slopes, then rise again, foot by foot, towards the upper walls, and to the peak piercing the azure heavens. There, without needing to repress the sensation of pride which I should have experienced in spite of myself upon the culminating apex of the mountain, I could enjoy the delight of feasting my gaze upon the beauties presented by the snow, the rocks, the forests, and pastures. I hovered half way up between the two zones of earth and sky, and I felt free without being isolated. Nowhere else could a sweeter sensation of peace fill my heart.

It is a great delight to attain a high point, overlooking a view of peaks, valleys, and plains. With what pleasure, what ecstasy of the senses, do we contemplate in one general panorama the enormous edifice of which we occupy the pinnacle! Beneath, upon the lower slopes, only one portion of the mountain is visible, or at most one side; but from the summit all the tops can be discerned down to the small hills and headlands of the base. As equals we gaze upon the encircling mountains; like them, our heads are in pure air and light; we soar to the free sky like an eagle whose flight bears him above the dull planet. At our feet, far below the peak, we behold that which the multitude beneath term the sky; they are clouds which, travelling slowly along the mountain's

sides, rend themselves upon the projecting angles of the
rocks and outskirts of the woods, leaving shreds of fog
here and there in the ravines, then, sailing away over the
plains, cast their great shadow upon the ground in ever-
varying form. From the top of this splendid observatory no rivers can be seen making their way like the
clouds whence they took their birth, but their motion is
revealed by the noisy uproar of the water heard afar off
from time to time, either issuing from the riven glaciers
or in the small lakes and cascades in the valley, **or mean-
dering** gently through the lower landscape. **In this**
scene of amphitheatres, ravines, gorges, dales, we **take
part, as if** we had suddenly become immortal, in the
great geological work of the excavating waters as they
empty their basins **in** every direction around the primi-
tive mass **of** the mountain. **We see them, so** to say, incessantly chiselling the enormous object so as to carry
away the débris wherewith to level the plain, to fill up
some ocean bay. I can distinguish that bay from the
summit on to which I have climbed; there below lies
extended that great abyss, the blue ocean, whence the
mountain has gone forth, and whither, sooner or later, it
must return.

As to man, he is invisible, but I imagine him. Like
nests half hidden in the branches, I can discern cottages,
hamlets, villages, dispersed in the valleys and upon the
sides of the verdant hills. **There** below, beneath the
smoke, under a layer of air vitiated by the breath of innumerable persons, something white indicates a large
city. The houses, the palaces, the lofty towers, the cupolas, all merge into one dirty, dingy color, which might
be described as a sort of mouldiness, contrasting with the

fresher **tints** of the surrounding country. Then I think sadly of all the perfidy and wickedness being enacted in that ant-hill, of all the vices fermenting beneath that almost invisible pustule; but, seen from the summit, the immense panorama of the country is beautiful as a whole, with its towns, villages, and isolated houses, which here and there brighten the scene beneath the light in which they are bathed; **the dark** spots˙blend with all that surrounds them in one harmonious whole; the atmosphere sheds its azure mantle **over the entire plain.**

Great is the difference between **the true form of our** picturesque mountain, **so rich** in its various **aspects, and that which I** ascribed **to it in my childhood when** looking at the maps which my tutor made me study; I then pictured to myself a perfectly regular isolated mass, sloping equally all round its circumference, gently rounded at the top, at the base slightly inflected and insensibly losing itself in the plains. There are no such mountains in the world. Even **the volcanoes which spring** up singly, far removed from any other groups, **and which** grow little **by little** as they eject cinders and lava sideways upon their declivities, do not possess that geometrical regularity. **The discharge of** these internal substances is sometimes produced **from the central crater,** sometimes from the **side** crevices; small subordinate volcanoes spring up here and there upon the slopes of the principal mountain, raising up heaps on its surface. Even the very wind labors to impart an irregular shape to it by causing the showers of cinders, vomited forth during the eruption, to fall according to its will.

But could we compare our mountain, an old witness of former ages, to a volcano, a mountain born yesterday,

and which, as yet, has hardly withstood the onslaughts
of weather? Ever since the day on which that corner
of the earth whereon we live assumed its first inequality,
destined to be gradually transformed into a mountain,
nature, which is the motive force, has labored without
relaxation to modify the aspect of that protuberance;
here it has raised up, elsewhere it has depressed, the
mass; made it bristle with peaks, studded it with cupolas and domes, has inclined, bent, excavated, chiselled,
toiled interminably at the ever-changing surface; and
now, even before our eyes, the task still goes on. To
the spirit which has watched the mountain during the
lapse of ages, it must have appeared as fluctuating, as
uncertain, as the ocean billows lashed by the storm; it is
a wave, a vapor; when it shall have disappeared, it will
be but as a dream.

Yet amid this changing or ever-varying ornamentation, produced by the continual action of the forces of
nature, the mountain does not cease to present a sort of
superb rhythm to any one who wanders about it, in order
to learn its construction. Whether the culminating portion is a broad plateau, a rounded mass, a vertical wall,
a ridge, an isolated pyramid, or even a cluster of distinct
needles, the whole mountain presents a general aspect
which harmonizes with that of the summit. From the
centre of the mass to the base of the mountain, other
peaks, or groups of subordinate peaks, succeed one another on every side; sometimes even at the foot of the
last chain which borders the alluvion of the plain or the
waters of the ocean, a miniature copy of the mountain
may be seen springing up as a small hillock, in the midst
of the fields, or as a rock out of the bosom of the waters.

"THE GREAT PEAK CAN BE SEEN RISING UP LIKE A PYRAMID."

The outlines of all these heights, succeeding one another as they incline gradually or abruptly, present a series of most graceful undulations. This sinuous line uniting the summits of the principal peak to the plain is the true slope—it is the road which a giant shod with magic boots would take.

The mountain which so long sheltered me is beautiful and serene beyond all others in the calm regularity of its features. From the highest pastures the great peak can be seen rising up like a pyramid of irregular tiers. The contrast of the whiteness of the patches of snow filling up the hollows impart to it a sombre, almost black, tint; but the green of the turf, covering the distant subordinate heights, appears all the softer in our sight; and our eyes, as they again travel down the enormous formidable-looking mass, rest with ecstasy upon the soft undulations of the pasture grounds: they are so graceful in their contour, so velvety in appearance, that we involuntarily think of the delight a giant would feel in caressing them with his hands. Farther down, abrupt declivities, rocky cliffs, and lower chains clad with woods, to a great extent conceal the mountain's sides from me; but the whole appears all the higher, the more sublime from the fact that my glance can only embrace one portion at a time, as it would a statue whose pedestal remains hidden; it is resplendent in the sky, in the region of clouds, in the pure light.

The beauty of the hollows, the chasms, the dales, or the defiles corresponds with that of every kind of peak and projection. Between the summit of our mountain and the next nearest point the crest dips considerably, and leaves a very easy passage between the two opposite

2

declivities. It is at this depression of the ridge that the first indentation of the open serpentine valley enters the two mountains. To this indentation others are added; then more again, scoring the surface of the rocks and meeting in ravines, which themselves converge towards a circle, whence, by a series of defiles and tiers of basins, the snow runs off and the waters descend into the valley.

Yonder, where the ground inclines very slightly, fields, clusters of common trees, groups of houses, begin to appear. On every side dales, some of a lovely, others of a severe aspect, bend towards the principal valley. Away beyond a distant turning, the valley disappears from our vision; but if we do lose sight of the bottom, at least we can imagine its general form and contour by the more or less parallel lines presented by the outlines of the lower chains. Taken as a whole, the valley, with its innumerable ramifications penetrating into the depths of the mountain, may be compared to trees whose thousands of branches are divided and subdivided into delicate twigs. It is by the form of the valley and all its network of dales that we can best understand the real elevation of the mountains separating them.

Do we not, from those summits whence our eyes can roam most freely over the country, see a great number of peaks which we compare one with another, and each of which enables us to understand the rest? Above the sinuous edge of the height rising from the yonder side of the valley a second outline of a range can be distinguished already assuming a bluish hue, and again beyond it a third or even a fourth series of azure mountains. These chains, which all eventually become attached to the great ridge of the principal summits, are but slightly parallel to one another, despite their indentations, and at one time appear to approach, then to recede, according to the freaks of the clouds and the progress of the sun. Twice a day the immense panorama of mountains is steadily unrolled, when the oblique morning and evening rays successively leave in the shadow that portion of **the ground turned towards** night, **and** bathe **in** light that which faces day. From the most distant western peaks to those which can hardly be distinguished in the east, there is one harmonious scale of every **color and** shade which can be produced by the effulgence of the sun and the transparency of the atmosphere. Among these mountains are some which a breath could efface, so ephemeral are they in tone, so delicately traced upon the sky, their background.

If but a slight vapor arises, an imperceptible mist forms on the horizon, or only the sun in its decline allows the shadows to increase, then these beautiful mountains, this snow, these glaciers, these pyramids, vanish by degrees, as in the twinkling of an eye. We beheld them in their splendor, and now they have disappeared from the sky; they are but a dream, a vague memory.

Chapter III.

ROCKS AND CRYSTALS.

The hard rock of the mountains, as well as that extending beneath the plains, is covered almost everywhere with a more or less deep layer of vegetable mould and with varieties of plants. Here there are forests, elsewhere brushwood, heather, whortleberries, furze ; in other places, again, and to the greatest extent, the short grass of pastures. Even where the rock appears naked, or juts out in points, or rises as a wall, the stone is clad with white, red, or yellow lichens, which often impart a similar appearance to rocks of the most different origin. Hardly ever, even in the cold regions of the summits, at . the foot of glaciers, and on the confines of the snow, does the stone appear without a cover of vegetation to disguise it. Sandstone, limestone, granite, to an unobservant traveller would seem to be of one and the same formation. Yet the diversity of the rocks is great. The mineralogist who wanders, hammer in hand, through the mountains may collect hundreds and thousands of stones differing in appearance, yet whose construction is intimately connected. Some are of a uniform grain throughout ; others are composed of different atoms, contrasting in shape, color, and brilliancy. Some are speckled, ridged, or grooved, transparent, translucent, and opaque. Some are to be seen bristling with crystals, with regular facets; others, again, are ornamented with arborizations, similar to bunches of tamarind or fern fronds. All kinds of metals are found in stones, whether in their pure state or mingled one with another; at one time they discover themselves as crystals or nodules, at others as simple fugitive erosions, similar to the brilliant reflections in a soap-bubble. Then, too, there are innumerable animal or vegetable fossils enclosed in the rock, and of which it retains the impression. As many separate fragments as there are, so many different evidences are to be found of the creatures which have existed during the incalculable series of past centuries.

Without being either a professional mineralogist or geologist, the traveller who understands how to look can perfectly see how wonderful is the diversity of rocks composing the mass of the mountain. Such is the contrast between the different parts of the vast edifice that, even from a distance, we can recognize to what formation they belong. From any isolated peak overlooking an extensive expanse, it is easy to distinguish the crest of the granite dome, the pyramid of slate, and the wall of calcareous rock.

It is in the immediate vicinity of the principal summit of our mountain that the granite best reveals itself. There a ridge of black rocks separates two fields of snow, spreading out their sparkling whiteness on either side. They might be described as a diadem of jet upon a muslin veil. It is by this ridge that it is easiest to gain the culminating point of the mountain, for there the crevasses, hidden beneath the uniform surface of the snow, are avoided. There we can plant our feet firmly upon

the ground, while by means of our arms we easily raise
ourselves up **step by step** in the steep places.   It was by
that route that **I** almost always made my ascent when,
leaving the flock and my companion the shepherd, I
went to spend some hours on the great peak.

Seen from a distance through the bluish vapors **of the**
atmosphere, the granite ridge appeared uniform enough.
The mountaineers, practical and almost shrewd in their
comparisons, term it a comb; indeed, it might be said to
be a row of regularly arranged pointed teeth; but when
in the midst of the **rock, we** find ourselves in a sort of
chaos; needles, tottering stones, heaped-up boulders,
strata superposed one above another, overhanging tow-
ers, walls propping themselves up against each other and
leaving narrow passages between them—such is the ridge
forming the angle of the mountain.   **Even** upon these
heights the rock is almost universally covered with **a**
coat of lichens; but in many places it has been laid bare
by the friction of ice, the moisture of the snow, the action of frosts, rain, wind, and the sun's rays.   Other
rocks, rent by thunder, have become magnetic from the
shock of the celestial fire.

In the midst of these ruins, it is easy to observe what,
until quite recently, was the interior of the rock.   I perceive crystals in all their brilliancy, white quartz, felspar
of a pale rose color, mica resembling a silver spangle.
In **other portions of the** mountain the exposed granite
presents **a fresh aspect: in** one rock it is white as marble, and sprinkled **over with** small black spots; else-
where it is blue and **sombre.**   Almost everywhere it is
very hard, and the slabs which might be cut out of it
would serve for the construction of lasting monuments;

but in other places it is so friable, the various crystals in it are so slightly aggregated, that a man can **easily crush** them between his fingers. A stream, taking its rise at the foot of a height composed of this so slightly cohesive material, spreads out in the ravine above a bed of the finest sand, all sparkling with mica. We might imagine that we beheld gold and silver gleaming through the rippling water. More than one rustic coming from the plains has been deceived, and has eagerly rushed upon the treasure, which the mocking stream carelessly sweeps away.

The incessant action of the snow and **water permits us** to observe another species of rock, which also exists to a great extent in the mass of the immense edifice. Not far **from the** ridges and domes of granite, which are the most elevated portions of the mountain, and seem, so to say, to be its core, another subordinate peak appears, whose aspect is of a remarkable regularity; it might be described as a four-sided pyramid, placed upon the enormous pedestal formed for it **by** the plateaux and declivities. It is a summit composed of slate rocks, which time, with all its atmospheric **changes** of wind, solar rays, snow, fog, and rain, incessantly pares away. The split slabs of slate become fissured, broken, and, in sliding masses, **roll** right down the slope. Sometimes a sheep's light step suffices to set myriads of stones in motion upon the whole side of a mountain.

Quite different from the slate is the calcareous rock, which forms some of the foremost crags. This rock, when broken, is **not shivered** into countless tiny fragments, but into great blocks. Such a fracture has rent a whole rock, three hundred yards high, from the base to

the summit; on either side we see the two vertical walls
reaching up to the sky; the light can hardly penetrate to
the bottom of the chasm, and the water wherewith it is
filled, and that has come down from the snowy heights,
only reflects the clearness from above in its seething rapids and the dashing spray of its cascades. Nowhere, not
even in mountains ten times as high, does nature appear
grander. From afar the calcareous portion of the mountain reassumes its true proportions, and we see that it is
commanded by much loftier rocky masses, but it always
surprises us by the mighty beauty of its layers and upright rocks, resembling Babylonian temples.

Very picturesque, although relatively of slight importance, are the sandstone and conglomerate rocks, composed of cemented fragments. In every part where the
incline of the ground favors the action of the water, the
latter tempers the cement and digs out a gutter for itself
—a narrow fissure, which in course of time ends by saw-
ing the rock in two. Other watercourses have similarly
dug out other fissures near the lesser ones, deeper in proportion to the greater abundance of the liquid mass borne
away; the rock thus cut in half at last resembles a labyrinth of obelisks, towers, and fortresses. Some of these
fragments of mountains now remind us of deserted towns,
with their damp, sinuous streets, crenellated walls, dungeons, overhanging towers, and curious statues. I still
recollect the impression of surprise bordering on fear
which I felt on approaching the opening of a gorge
already invaded by the shades of evening. Afar off I
perceived the black fissure; but beside the entrance on
the summit of the mountain I also remarked strange
forms, which looked like giants in a row. They were

high columns of clay, each bearing upon its apex a great round stone, which from a distance seemed to be a head; the rain had by degrees dissolved and washed away the surrounding soil, but the ponderous stones had been respected, and by their weight continued to impart consistency to the gigantic pillars of clay supporting them.

Every crag, every rock belonging to the mountain, thus has its own peculiar aspect, according to the material composing it and its power of resisting the elements of decay. Thus arises an infinite variety of forms, which is still more increased by the contrast presented to the exterior of the rocks by the snow, grass, forests, and cultivation. The picturesqueness of the lines and ground is augmented by the continual changes of ornamentation undergone by the surface. And yet how very few in number are the elements composing the mountain, and which by their mixture impart to it this prodigious variety of aspects!

The chemists, who in their laboratories analyze the rock, teach us what is the composition of these different crystals. They tell us that quartz is silica, that is to say, oxide of silicon, a metal which, in its purer state, resembles silver, and when mixed with the oxygen of the air has become a whitish rock. They also tell us that felspar, mica, augite, hornblende, and other crystals which are found in such great variety in the rocks of the mountain, are composites, in which other minerals, aluminium, potassium, are again found with silicon, united with the atmospheric gases in varying proportions, and following certain laws of chemical affinity. Every mountain —those near at hand as well as distant ones—the plains at their base, and all the whole earth are but metal in

an impure state; if the fused **and** mingled elements of
the mass of the globe were suddenly to resume their purity, the planet would, for the inhabitants of Mars and
Venus levelling their telescopes at us, possess the appearance of **a silver** ball revolving in a black sky.

The geologist, who seeks to discover the elements of
stones, often finds that all **the** massive rocks composed of
crystals or crystalline paste consist, as does granite, of
oxidized metals; such are porphyry, serpentine, and the
igneous rocks which have issued from the earth during
volcanic explosions; trachyte, basalt, obsidian, **pumice-**
stone: all these come from silicon, aluminium, potassium, sodium, calcium.   As to the rocks disposed in planes
or strata, placed in layers the one above another, why
should they not also be metals, since they, to a great extent, result from **the disaggregation and** redistribution of
the massive **rocks? Stones** crushed to pieces, then cemented again, sand adhering to the rocks after **having**
been ground and pulverized, clay that has become compact after having been tempered by water, slates (which
are nothing more than hardened clay), are almost all the
remains of earlier rocks, and, like them, are composed of
metal.   Limestone alone, which constitutes so considerable a portion of the earth's crust, does not proceed directly from the destruction of the most ancient rocks; it
is formed of the débris which has passed through the
organism of marine animals: they have been eaten and
digested, but are none the less metallic; their foundation
is calcium combined with sulphur, carbon, and phosphorus.   Thus, thanks to the mixture, the varied and changing combinations, the polished, uniform, impenetrable
mass of metal has assumed bold and picturesque forms,

has hollowed itself **into** basins for lakes and rivers, has **clothed** itself again with vegetable mould, and has ended **by** entering even into the sap of plants and the blood of animals.

The pure metal reveals itself here and there in other places amid the stones of the mountain. In the midst of landslips and on the edges of springs ferruginous masses are often to be seen; crystals of iron, copper, lead, combined with other elements, are found in the scattered remains; sometimes a particle of gold gleams in the sand of the stream. But in hard rocks neither the precious mineral nor crystals are distributed at haphazard; they are disposed in ramified veins, which are especially developed between beds of different formations. These lodes of metal, like the magic thread of the labyrinth, have led miners, and after them geologists, into the depths and history of the mountain.

Formerly, so legends tell us, it was easy to collect all these riches **of** the interior of the mountain; all that a man needed was a little luck and the favor of the gods. If he made a false step, he would catch hold of a shrub to save himself. The fragile stem gave way, dragging with it a great stone that concealed **a** hitherto unknown cave. The shepherd boldly forced his way into the opening, not without uttering some magic formula or touching some amulet; then, after having walked along **in** the dark passage for a long time, he suddenly found himself beneath a vaulted roof of crystals and diamonds; statues of gold **and** silver, profusely ornamented with rubies; topaz and sapphires adhered to every side of the apartment; he needed but to stoop to gather up the treasures. Not by simple incantations or without trouble

can man in our days succeed in obtaining gold or other
metals lying dormant in the rocks.   The precious particles are rare, impure, mingled with earth, and far the
greatest portion do not assume their brilliancy and value
until after they have passed through the refining-fur-
nace.

Chapter IV.

THE ORIGIN OF THE MOUNTAIN.

Thus, down to its very smallest atom, the enormous mountain presents a combination of divers elements, which are mingled in varying proportions; every crystal, every mineral, every grain of sand or particle of limestone, has its endless history, just as have the stars themselves. Like the universe, the smallest fragment of rock possesses its genesis; but, while mutually aiding one another by science, the physician, chemist, astrologist, and geologist are still anxiously asking themselves if they do thoroughly understand this stone and the mystery of its origin.

And is it certain that they have unveiled the origin of the mountain? When we see all these rocks—sandstone, limestone, slate, and granite—can we tell how the prodigious mass accumulated and rose up towards the sky? While contemplating it in its superb beauty, can we weak dwarfs, who look on, examine ourselves, and say to the mountain, with the conscious pride of satisfied intelligence, "The least of your stones can crush us, but yet we understand you; we know what was your birth, what your history?"

As much as, and even more than, we do children ask questions on beholding nature and its phenomena; but,

in their simple confidence, they almost always content
themselves with the vague and untruthful reply given
by a father or an elder who does not know, or by a professor who pretends to be ignorant of nothing. If they
did not receive this reply, they would go on searching
forever, until they had discovered for themselves some
kind of an explanation, for a child cannot remain in
doubt; entering triumphantly upon life full of the sentiment of his existence, it is necessary that he should
be able to speak like an authority upon every subject.
Nothing ought to remain unknown to him.

In the same manner, nations who had just emerged
from their pristine barbarism found for themselves a
definitive explanation for everything that impressed
them. The first explanation, that which best responded
to their intelligence and the habits of their race, was
approved. Transmitted from lip to lip, the legend ended by becoming the divine word, and a tribe of inter-
preters rose up to give it the support of their moral
authority and ceremonies. It is thus that in the mythical heritage of almost every nation we find accounts
which relate to us the birth of the mountains, rivers,
earth, ocean, plants, animals, and even of man himself.

The most simple explanation is that which shows us
the gods and genii hurling mountains down from heav-
en, and allowing them to fall by chance, or else raising
them up and rebuilding them carefully like the columns
destined to bear the vaults of the skies. Thus were
constructed Libanus and Hermon; thus was Mount At-
las with those stalwart shoulders planted at the ends of
the earth. Elsewhere, when once they were created, the
mountains frequently changed their places, and the gods

utilized them **for the** discharge **of** their thunderbolts. The Titans, who were not gods, threw down all the mountains of Thessaly in order to use them again **for** building up the ramparts round Olympus ; even gigantic Athos was not too weighty for their arms ; they carried it from the heart of Thracia into the middle of the sea to the spot where it stands erect at this present day. A giantess of the North had filled her apron with little hills, and dropped them at certain distances, that she might recognize her way. Vishnu, one day seeing a young girl asleep beneath the sun's too ardent rays, took up a mountain and held it poised upon his fingertips **to** shelter the beautiful sleeper. This, the legend tells us, was the origin of sunshades.

Nor was it even always necessary for gods and giants to lift up the mountains in order to remove them ; the latter obeyed a mere sign. Stones hastened to listen to the strains of Orpheus's lyre, mountains stood erect to hear Apollo ; it was thus that Helicon, the home of the Muses, took its birth. The prophet Mohammed arrived two thousand years too late. Had he been born in **an** age of a simpler faith, he would **not** have gone to the mountain ; it would have gone to him.

Side by side with this explanation of the mountain's birth by the will of the gods, the mythology of many nations furnishes another less extravagant. According to this idea, the rocks and mountains would be animate organisms put forth naturally upon the earth's huge body as is the stamen in the corolla of a flower. While, on the one side, the ground descended to receive the waters of the ocean, on the other it rose up towards the sun to welcome its vivifying light. It is thus that the plants raise their stems and turn their petals towards the planet, looking down upon them and imparting to them their brilliancy. But the ancient legends have lost their believers, and are merely poetical recollections for mankind; they have retired to join other dreams; and the spirits of inquirers, emancipated from these illusions, have become more eager in their pursuit after truth. The men of our days, too, like those of ancient times, have still to repeat, while contemplating the peaks gilded by the light, " How were they able to raise themselves up to the sky ?"

Even in our time, when learned men profess to base their theories upon observation and experience only, many fancies sufficiently resembling the legends of the ancients as to the origin of the mountains still exist. One big modern book endeavors to demonstrate to us that the sun's light which bathes our planet had become solidified, and had condensed itself into table-lands and mountains all over the earth. Another declares that the attraction of the sun and moon, not content twice a day to lift up the waves of the sea, has also caused the earth to swell, and has carried up the solid waves to the regions of snow. Finally, another tells us how the comets which have wandered astray in the heavens have come to collide with our globe, have pierced holes in its crust as stones shatter a piece of ice, and have caused the mountains to burst forth in long ranges and groups.

Happily the earth, always toiling at fresh creations, does not cease to labor before our eyes, and shows us how by degrees it alters the rugosities of its surface. It destroys, but it also reconstructs, itself daily; constantly it levels some mountains to raise up others, hollows out

"HOW WERE THEY ABLE TO RAISE THEMSELVES UP TO THE SKIES?"

valleys just to fill them up again. While wandering over the surface of the globe, and carefully observing its natural phenomena, we can see how hills and mountains are formed—slowly, it is true, and not by any sudden upheaval, as the lovers of the marvellous would have it to be. We see them take their birth either directly from the bosom of the earth, or indirectly, so to say, by the erosion of plateaux, just as a block of marble gradually assumes the form of a statue. When an insular or continental mass, some hundreds or thousands of yards high, receives rain in abundance, its slopes gradually become indented with ravines, dales, valleys; the uniform surface of the plateau is cut into peaks, ridges, pyramids; scooped out into amphitheatres, basins, precipices; systems of mountains appear by degrees whereever the level ground has rolled down to any enormous extent. It is the same in those portions of the earth where a plateau assailed by rain on one side only is cut up into mountains merely on that slope; thus is in Spain that terrace of La Mancha where it descends towards Andalusia by the escarpments of the Sierra Morena.

In addition to these external causes which change plateaux into mountains, slow transformations in the interior of the earth are also being accomplished, bringing about vast excavations. Those hard-working men who, hammer in hand, go about for many years among the mountains in order to study their form and structure, observe, in the lower beds of marine formation which constitute the non-crystalline portion of the mountains, gigantic rents or fissures extending thousands of yards in length. Masses, millions of yards thick, have been completely raised up again by these shocks, or turned as

completely upside down, so that what was formerly the
surface has now become the bottom. The beds giving
way in consequence of successive shocks have bared the
skeleton of crystalline rocks which they enveloped as if
with a mantle; they have exposed the core of the mountain, as a curtain suddenly drawn aside discovers a hidden statue.

But such falling-away has been of less importance
than has plication in the history of the earth and the
mountains forming its external inequalities. Subjected
to slow secular pressure, the rock, the clay, the layers
of sandstone, the veins of metal, can all be folded up
like a piece of cloth, and the folds thus formed become
mountains and valleys. The earth's surface, similarly to
that of the ocean, is stirred up into waves; but these undulations are of a very different magnitude: the Andes,
the Himalayas, for instance, thus rear themselves up
again above the level of the plains. The rocks of the
earth find themselves constantly subjected to these lateral impulsions, which fold and refold them in different
directions, keeping the beds incessantly in a state of
fluctuation. It is thus that the skin of fruit becomes
wrinkled.

The peaks which rise straight up from the ground
and gradually climb from the level of the sea towards
the frigid altitudes of the atmosphere are mountains of
lava and volcanic cinders. In many parts of the terrestrial surface they can easily be studied rising, growing
before the naked eye. Differing vastly from ordinary
mountains, volcanoes, properly so called, are perforated
by a central crater through which the smoke and pulverized fragments of burnt rock escape; but when they

become extinguished the crater closes, and the slopes of
the volcanic cone, whose outline loses its pristine regularity beneath the influence of rains and vegetation, end
by resembling those of other mountains. Elsewhere
there are rocky masses which, rising out of the bosom
of the earth either in a liquid or pulpy state, simply
issue from a long fissure in the ground, and are not
thrown up by a crater as are the scoriæ of Vesuvius
and Etna. The lava, accumulating in peaks and branch-
ing out into promontories, merely differs by its youth
from those old hoary-headed mountains with which other portions of the earth's surface bristle. The lava, once
boiling, gradually cools; it flows into fresh beds outside,
and clothes itself anew with vegetable mould; it receives the rain in its interstices, sending it forth again
as streamlets and rivers; finally, it is covered once more
at its base with new geological formations, and becomes
surrounded, like the other mountains, with layers of
gravel, sand, or clay. In course of time, all that the
geologist's eye can discover is that they have sprung out
of the bosom of that great furnace, the earth, as if a
mass of fused metal.

Among these ancient mountains, forming a portion of
those groups and systems termed the "vertebral columns" of the continents, are many composed of rocks
very similar to actual lava, and of an analogous chemical
formation. The greatest portion of the granite rocks
seem to be formed in the same manner as these lavas
—porphyries, traps, and melaphyres—which have issued
from the earth through wide fissures, and have spread
out over the ground like a viscous substance, which
would soon congeal on coming into contact with the air.

They, as well as lava, **are** crystalline, and their crystals
contain the same simple substances in their elements,
silicium and aluminium. Is it not reasonable to suppose that granite has also been a paste-like mass, and the
crevices of the ground have afforded a passage to its
boiling streams? All the same, this is but an hypothesis
now under discussion, and not a demonstrated truth. **It**
is believed that as the lava, which springs out of the
earth, sometimes lifts up strips of ground with its forests or fields, so have eruptions of granite or similar rocks
been the most frequent cause of the upheaval of strata
of various formations constituting the most considerable
portion of the mountains. Strata of lime, sandstone, and
clay, which the waters of the sea or of a lake had once
deposited in parallel layers upon the bottom of their
bed, and which had become the external pellicle of
the earth, would have been thus bent down and set up
again by the mass rising out of the depths in search of
a means of egress. Here the swelling wave of granite
would have broken the upper strata into isles and islands,
all of which, disconnected, split up, crumpled into vari-
ous folds, are now dispersed among the depressions and
upon the points of the upheaving rock; elsewhere the
granite would have opened but one crevice for its passage through the ground, by folding back on either side
the outer layers, following the inclination of the most
varied angles; again, in other places the granite, without
even reaching daylight, would none the less have thrown
out hummocks on the upper strata. These, under the
pressure which had **caused them** to become folded, would
have ceased to be **plains, in order to be transformed** into
hills and mountains. **Thus even the** heights formed of

strata, quietly deposited **at** the bottom of the waters, **could have** erected themselves into peaks, **in the same** manner as the protuberances **of** lava ; a well dug **through** the superposed beds would reach the nucleus of porphyry or granite.

While admitting that most of the mountains have made their appearance in the same manner as those of lava, the cause, inducing all these substances to burst from the earth in a state of fusion, still remains a **subject** for reflection. Ordinarily people suppose that it **has** been explained, so to say, by the contraction of the outer crust of the globe, which slowly **cooled while** radiating heat into space. **Formerly our** planet was a drop of **burning metal.** While rolling through the cold firmament it has gradually become congealed. But is it the shell alone that has become solidified, as people love to say, or has the whole drop been rendered hard, down to its very core ? As yet this is not known, for there is nothing to prove that the lava of our volcanoes issues from an immense reservoir, supplying all the interior of the globe. We only know that sometimes the lava forces itself through the crevices of the ground, and flows to the surface, just as the granite, porphyry, and other similar rocks are said to have flowed out of fissures in the terrestrial bark, as the sap escapes through a wound in a plant. The tide of shattered stones is said to have risen from the interior, under the pressure of the planetary crust, gradually to be once more contracted by its own process of cooling.

Chapter V.

FOSSILS.

Whatsoever may be the primary origin of the mountain, its history has at least been known to us ever since a period greatly anterior to the annals of our human race. One hundred and fifty generations of man have barely succeeded one another since the first acts of our ancestors were accomplished, evidences of whom have remained; before that period the existence of our race has only been revealed to us by doubtful monuments. The inanimate history of the mountain, on the contrary, has been written in visible characters for millions of centuries.

The great work, that which even struck our forefathers ever since the infancy of civilization, and which they related in various ways in their legends, is that the rocks, distributed in regular layers, the one above another, like the stones of a building, have been deposited by the waters. Let any person walk along the edge of a river, look at the temporary gutter formed in the depressions of the soil, and he will see the current seize upon gravel, grains of sand, dust, and all the scattered detritus, to distribute them in order upon the bottom and shores of its bed; the heaviest fragments will be disposed in layers at those spots where the water loses some of the rapidity of

"UPON THE ROCKY SHORES OF THE OCEAN."

its first impetus, the lighter molecules will proceed farther, spreading themselves in beds upon the smooth surface, and finally the tenuous clay, whose weight hardly
exceeds that of the water, will settle down in layers
wherever the torrent-like motion of the water stops.
Upon the shores, and in the basins of lakes and seas, the
layers of débris deposited successively are still much
more regular, for those waters do not possess the impet-
uous motion of running streams, and everything received
by their surface is sifted through the depth of their
stationary waters, without anything occurring to disturb
the equable action of the waves and currents.

It is thus that in this vast nature the division of labor
is arranged. Upon the rocky shores of the ocean, beaten
by the waves of the offing, we see nothing but gravel
and heaped-up boulders. Elsewhere, stretching away
beyond our sight, are beaches of fine sand, upon which
the tidal waves roll up in volutes of foam. Those who
take soundings to study the floor of the sea tell us that
upon vast extents, as large as provinces, the remains
which their instruments bring up are always composed
of a uniform mud, more or less mixed with clay or sand,
according to the different latitudes. They have also
proved that in other portions of the ocean the rock
formed at the bottom of the marine bed is of pure chalk.
Shells, spicules of sponge, animalculæ of all descriptions,
inferior organisms, silicious or calcareous, fall incessantly,
like rain, from the surface waters, and become mingled
with the innumerable creatures which multiply, live,
and die on the bottom in sufficiently great numbers to
constitute strata as deep as those of our mountains; but,
then, are not these formed of detritus of the same kind?

In an unknown future, when the actual abysses of the ocean shall be extended as plains, or rise up again as peaks in the sun's light, our descendants will behold geological portions of ground similar to those which we see to-day, and which, perhaps, may have disappeared, cut up into fragments by the flowing waters.

During the course of ages, the strata of marine and lacustrine formation, of which the greatest part of our mountain is composed, have succeeded in occupying, at a great elevation above the sea, their sloping, contorted, and curiously folded position. Whether they have been upheaved by pressure from below, or whether the ocean has receded in consequence of the earth becoming congealed and contracted, or else from some totally different cause, and that in this manner it had left layers of sand and limestone upon the ancient shoals, which have since become continents, there these layers are now, and we can study at our leisure the remains which many of them have brought up from the submarine world.

These remains are fossils, the débris of plants and animals preserved in the rock. It is true that the molecules composing the framework, animal or vegetable, of these bodies have disappeared with the tissue of the flesh and the drops of blood or sap; but the whole has been replaced by particles of stone which have kept the form and even the color of the creature destroyed. Within the thickness of these stones, shells of mollusks, disks, spheres, spines, cylinders, silicious and calcareous bits of stick, of foraminifera and diatoms, are to be met with in astounding numbers; but we also find forms which exactly correspond with the soft flesh of the creatures of these organizations; we see the skeletons of fish with their fins and scales; recognize the wing-sheaths of insects, twigs and leaves, even footprints can be distinguished; upon the hard rock, too, which was formerly the shifting sand of the beach, we find the impression of drops of rain, and the intersecting ripple-marks traced by the wavelets on the shore.

Fossils very rare in certain rocks of marine formation, very numerous, on the contrary, in other strata, and constituting almost the entire mass of marble and chalk, help us to recognize the relative age of the strata which have been deposited in the course of time All the fossiliferous beds, indeed, have not been turned upside down, or curiously mixed up by excavations and landslips; most of them have even preserved their regular superposition, so that the fossils can be studied and collected in the order in which they appeared. Where the strata, still in their normal condition, maintain the position they formerly occupied after having been deposited by the maritime or lacustrine waters, the shells discovered in the upper bed are certainly more modern than those of the layers situated lower down. ˙ Hundreds, thousands of years, represented by innumerable intermediate atoms of lime or sandstone, have separated the two epochs of existence.

If the same species of plants and animals had always lived upon the earth, ever since the day on which these animate organisms made their first appearance upon the congealed crust of the planet, we should not have been able to judge of the relative age of the two terrestrial strata, separated one from the other. But different creatures have not ceased to succeed one another for many ages, and consequently, also, in the superposed

strata. Certain forms which may be seen in great abundance in the heart of the most ancient stratified rocks
gradually become rarer in those of less remote origin,
and then end by disappearing altogether. The new species which succeed the first have also, like every individual creature, their period of regeneration, propaga-
tion, decay, and death; every species of animal or vegetable fossil might be compared to a gigantic tree whose
roots plunge into the lower domains of ancient formation, and whose trunk becomes ramified, finally losing
itself in the higher strata of more recent origin.

Those geologists who, in different countries of the
world, spend their time in examining and studying the
rocks, molecule by molecule, in order to discover in them
vestiges of once living creatures, have been able, thanks
to the order of succession of every species of fossil, to
recognize in the imprisoned remains the relative age of
the different strata of the earth deposited by the waters.
Ever since sufficiently numerous observations have been
compared with one another, it is even frequently easy,
on seeing a single fossil, to pronounce to what epoch of
terrestrial ages belongs the rock in which it was found.
Any specimen whatever of limestone, schist, or sandstone, showing a clear impression of shell or plant, will
often suffice. The naturalist, without any fear of being
mistaken, declares that the stone in which the impression
is marked belongs to such and such a series of rocks, and
ought to be classified in such and such an epoch in the
planet's history.

These testimony - bearing fossils, which in an animate
form moved, millions of years ago, in the mud of oceanic
abysses, are now met with again at every height in the

mountain strata. They are to be seen on most of the
Pyrenean peaks; they constitute whole Alps; they are
recognized upon the Caucasus and Cordilleras. Equally would man see them on the summits of the Himalaya if he could attain those altitudes. Nor is this all;
these fossiliferous beds, which to - day pass beyond the
middle zone of the clouds, formerly reached much more
considerable elevations. In many places, upon one side
of a mountain, it is shown that the strata of rocks are
more or less frequently interrupted. Here and there,
perhaps, the geologist may again find some portions of
these beds, but they do not continue to any extent until
much farther away upon the opposite side of the mountain. What has become of the intermediate fragments?
They existed formerly, for, even when breaking through
them, the granite mass rising out of the interior could
only split them, but none the less have the cracked strata
remained upon the slippery summit. .

Chapter VI.

THE DESTRUCTION OF THE PEAKS.

AND yet these enormous masses, mountains piled upon mountains, have passed away like clouds swept along the sky by the wind; the strata four or five thousand yards thick, which the geological section of rocks shows us had formerly existed, have disappeared to enter into the circuit of a new creation. It is true that the mountain still appears formidable to us, and we contemplate with admiration, mingled with alarm, the superb peaks penetrating far away beyond the clouds, into the icy atmosphere of space. So lofty are these snow-clad pyramids that they conceal one half of the sky from us; from below, their precipices, which in vain our glance tries to grasp, make us dizzy. Yet all this is but a ruin—mere débris.

Formerly the strata of slates, limestone, sandstone, which rested against the base of the mountain, and here and there raised themselves up into secondary summits, would meet again above the top of the granite in uniform layers; they added their enormous thickness to the already great height of the topmost peak. The altitude of the mountain was doubled; the apex then attained that region in which the atmosphere is so rarefied that even an eagle's wings no longer possess the power to support him. It is not now our glance, it is our imagination that is filled with dread at the thought of what this mountain then was, and of what the snow, the frosts, the rains, and the storms have swept away from it in the course of ages. What infinite history, what vicissitudes without number, in the succession of plants, animals, and man since the mountains have thus changed their form and lost the half of their height!

This prodigious work of paring away could not be accomplished without, in many places, leaving unexceptionable traces behind. The débris which, with the snow, has slipped from the top of the peaks, driven down before it by the ice, having been triturated, pared, carried away as boulders, gravel, and sand by the waters, has not always returned to the sea, whence, at an anterior period, it came forth; enormous accumulations are still to be seen in the space that separates the bold declivities of the mountains from the low lands bordering on the ocean. In this intermediate zone, in which the smaller hills run out in long undulations like the waves of the sea, the soil is entirely composed of rolled-down stones and heaped-up gravel. All are the remains of the mountain, reduced by the water into minute fragments, transported in small quantities, and poured out in vast alluvions at the mouths of large valleys. The torrents, descended from the heights, excavate at their leisure these plateaux of débris, causing the talus to slip down the indentations which they have dug out. On the slopes of the deep ditch, with its winding stream, the divers rocks which provided the materials for the great edifice, the mountain, are to be seen in the most glaring confusion : here are blocks of granite and fragments of porphyry; there are schists, with sharp ridges, half buried in the

3*

sand; in other places are pieces of quartz, sandstone, boulders of limestone, lumps of mineral ore, dull crystals. Also are to be found fossils of different periods, and, in those openings in which the waters have so long been eddying round, many skeletons of floating animals have been arrested. It is there that by thousands were discovered bones of the hippalion, urus, elk, rhinoceros, mastodon, mammoth, and other great mammalia, which formerly wandered about our fields, and have now disappeared, yielding to man the dominion of the world. The same torrents which brought all these remains carry them away again piece by piece, reducing them to powder; skeletons and fossils, clay and sand, blocks of schist, of sandstone, and porphyry, all give way by degrees—all wend their way to the sea; the immense work of denudation, which has been accomplished in the great mountain, commences again on a small scale with the accumulations of rubbish; hollowed out into ravines by the water, they gradually fall away in height—they break up into distinct hills. Nevertheless, even diminished as it is by the work of centuries, all crumbling and ruined, the plateau of detritus, extended at the base of the mountain, would suffice to add some thousands of yards to the principal peak, if it were to resume its first position in the strata of rock. "It is by licking the mountains," says an ancient prayer of the Hindoos, "that the celestial cow" (that is to say, the rain from heaven) "formed the fields."

Under our very eyes the work of denudation of the rocks goes on with surprising activity. We see mountains, composed of very incoherent materials, melt, dissolve, so to say; gorges are hollowed out in the sides of the mountain, breaches opened in the centre of the crest; furrowed by avalanches and floods, the great mass, so lately compact and solitary, by degrees becomes divided into two distinct peaks, apparently retreating from one another as the excavation of the separating gulf extends farther and farther down.

Especially in the spring, when the ground has been saturated with the melting snow, landslips, subsidence, and erosion assume such proportions that the whole mountain seems to desire to sink down and to take its way into the plain. One damp, warm day, I had ventured into one of the mountain gorges to look at the snow once more before the waters of spring should have swept it away. It still obstructed the bottom of the ravine, but in many places it was unrecognizable, to such an extent was it covered with black débris and mixed up with mud. The slate-colored rocks commanding the gorge seemed to be changed into a sort of pulp, and to have sunk down in great lumps; the black mire oozing in streamlets out of the walls of the defile was pouring with a dull rumbling sound into the semi-liquid snow. On every side I beheld nothing but cataracts of sullied snow and débris; instinctively I asked myself, in a sort of alarm, if the rocks, melting like the snow, would not unite at the head of the valley in one viscous mass and make their escape right down the country? The torrent, which I perceived here and there through holes, to the bottom of which the upper beds of snow had fallen, appeared to be transformed into a river of ink, so heavily were its waters laden with detritus; it was one enormous mass of mud in motion. Instead of the clear, joyous sound I had been accustomed to hear, the torrent sent

forth one continual roar, arising from the rubbish revolving on the bottom of the bed. It is in spring especially, at the period of the earth's annual renovation,
that we see this prodigious work of destruction carried
out.

In addition to this, an immense amount of invisible
labor goes on inside the stone. All the changes caused
by the weather are but external modifications; the internal transformations accomplished in the molecules of
rock have at least equally important results. While the
mountain displaces its stones on the exterior and incessantly changes its aspect, in the interior it assumes a new
structure, and even the composition of the strata becomes
modified. Taken in its *ensemble,* the mountain is an immense natural laboratory in which all the physical and
chemical forces are at work, making use of time, that
sovereign agent which man has not at his disposal, in order to accomplish their task.

In the first place, the enormous weight of the mountain, equivalent to hundreds of thousands of tons, presses
so powerfully upon the lower rocks as to impart to many
of them a very different appearance from that which
they possessed on emerging from the sea. Little by little, beneath this formidable pressure, the slates and other
schistous formations assume a leaf-like structure. While
thousands and thousands of centuries are passing away,
the compressed molecules grow into thinner leaflets,
which eventually can be easily separated, when, after
some geological revolution, the rock once more finds itself brought to the surface. The action of the earth's
heat, up to a certain distance at least, increases with the
depth, and also contributes to changing the structure of

the rocks. It is thus that the limestones have been transformed into marble.

But not only do the molecules of the rock approach
or retire from one another, group themselves diversely
according to the physical conditions in which they find
themselves during the course of ages, but the composition of the stones changes equally; it is one continual
crossing backward and forward—an incessant travelling
to and fro of the bodies which displace, become mixed
up with, and follow one another. The water which penetrates through all the fissures into the thickness of the
mountain, and that which rises up again in vapors from
the profound abysses, serves as the principal vehicle for
those elements, at one time attracting, then repelling one
another, which are drawn down into the great vortex of
geological life. One crystal is driven out by another
from the fissures of the mountain; iron, copper, silver,
or gold replace the clay and hot lime; the dull rock becomes irisated with the multitude of substances penetrating it. By the displacement of carbon, sulphur, and
phosphorus, the lime becomes marl, dolomite, plaster,
gypsum, crystalline; in consequence of these new combinations, the rock expands or contracts, and revolutions
are slowly accomplished in the bosom of the mountain.
Soon the stone, compressed into too narrow a space, up-
heaves, scatters the superincumbent strata, causes enormous pieces to fall away, and, by slow efforts, whose results are the same as those of a prodigious explosion,
gives a new arrangement to the rocks of the mountain.
At one time the stone contracts, splits, hollows itself out
into grottos and galleries; a great downfall takes place,
thus modifying the exterior aspect and form of the

mountain. At every internal modification in the composition of the rock, a corresponding change takes place
outside. In itself the mountain recapitulates every geological revolution. It has grown during thousands of
centuries, diminished during other thousands, and in its
strata all the phenomena of increase and decrease, of
formation and destruction, which are accomplished on a
larger scale in the great earth succeed one another without end. The history of the mountain is that of the
planet itself; it is one unceasing destroying, one endless
building-up again.

Every rock recapitulates a geological period. In this
mountain, so graceful in its outline, the earth springs up
so grandly that any one would believe it to be the work
of one day, such unity does its whole form betray, so
thoroughly do the details coincide with the general harmony. And yet a myriad of centuries has been spent
in modelling this mountain. Here some ancient granite
tells of past ages in which the vegetable fibre had not yet
covered the terrestrial scoriæ. The gneiss itself, only
formed at a time when plants and animals were yet un-
born, tells us that when the ocean deposited it upon the
shores mountains had already been demolished by the
waves. The slab of slate, preserving the bones or merely a slight impression of some animal, relates the history
of innumerable generations which have followed one another upon the surface of the earth in the never-ending
battle of life; the traces of coal speak to us of immense
forests, each one of which, in dying, has made but one
thin carboniferous layer; the white chalk, an accumulation of animalcula, which the microscope reveals to us,
enables us to take part in the work of multitudes of or-

ganisms swarming at the bottom of the sea; the remains of every species show us the water of the rains, the snow, the glaciers, the torrents sweeping down the mountains in former times just as they do at the present day, and from age to age changing the scene of their activity.

At the thought of all these revolutions, these incessant transformations, this continued series of phenomena produced in the mountain, of the part it plays in the general life of the earth and in the history of mankind, we comprehend the first poets, who, at the foot of the Pamir or Bolor, related those myths whence all others are derived. They tell us that the mountain is a creator. It is the mountain that pours into the plains the fertilizing waters, and sends them the nourishing mud. The mountain it is that, with the sun's aid, brings to life the plants, animals, and man; it is the mountain which decks the desert with flowers and sows it with happy cities. According to an ancient Hellenic legend, it was Eros who caused the mountains to rise up and modelled the earth—that god of everlasting youth, the first-born of Chaos; that nature which renews itself unceasingly, the god of eternal love.

Chapter VII.

LANDSLIPS.

Not only is the mountain being incessantly transformed into plains by the erosions which the rains; the frosts, the slippery snow, the avalanches, cause it to undergo, but even many fragments break away with a violent and sudden fall. Similar catastrophes are frequent in those portions of the mountain in which the erect or overhanging strata are widely separated from one another by materials of a different nature, which the water can wash away or dissolve. When these intermediate substances disappear, the strata, deprived of support, must sooner or later subside into the valley. These fallen débris form a knoll, a hill, or even a secondary mountain by the side of the greater escarpments.

One stately peak, which I loved to climb on account of its isolation and the proud beauty of its crests, had always appeared to me, like the great summit itself, to be an independent rock, clinging, by its deep layers, to the subjacent earth; yet it was but a huge piece detached from a neighboring mountain. I recognized this, one day, from the position of the strata and from the appearance of the marks still visible on the broken parts of the two corresponding walls. The mass which had fallen down, and now bore hamlets and fields, woods and pastures, had only needed, after the rupture, to pivot its base and turn over upon itself. One of its faces had been buried in the soil, while on the other side it had been partially uprooted. In its fall it had closed up the outlet of an entire valley, and the torrent, formerly flowing peacefully in the bottom, had been obliged to transform itself into a lake, in order to fill up the valley in which it was imprisoned, and whence it descends once more, at this very time, by a succession of rapids and cascades. No doubt these changes took place before the country was inhabited, for the tradition of the event has not been preserved. It is geology that teaches the peasant the history of his own mountain.

As to the landslips of minor importance, the fall of rocks, which, without sensibly changing the aspect of the country, none the less lay waste the pastures and demolish the villages with their inhabitants, the mountaineers do not need us to describe them; unhappily, they have too often witnessed these terrible occurrences. Ordinarily, they receive a warning some short time before. That part which has been pushed out of the interior of the mountain in labor causes the stone incessantly to vibrate from the top to the very foundations of the walls. Little half-loosened fragments first become detached, and bound down the whole length of the slopes. Heavier masses, carried away in their turn, follow the lesser stones by taking, like them, great leaps into space. Then come whole lumps of rock; everything that must give way breaks the bonds which attached it to the interior skeleton of the mountain, and with one blow the fearful hail-storm of boulders crashes down upon the troubled plain. The hubbub is indescribable; it is like

a battle among a hundred tempests. Even in broad daylight the débris of the rocks, mingled with the dust, the
vegetable mould, the fragments of plants, totally ob-
scured the sky; sometimes evil-boding flashes of lightning, proceeding from the rocks, hurled against one another, burst through this gloom. After the storm, when
the mountain has ceased to dash its severed rocks into
the plain, when the atmosphere has cleared again, the
inhabitants of the country which is spared come to contemplate the disaster. Cottages and gardens, enclosures
and pastures, have disappeared beneath the hideous chaos
of stones; there, too, are friends, relatives, sleeping their
last sleep. The mountaineers have told me that in their
valley one village, twice destroyed by avalanches of
stones, has been rebuilt a third time upon the same site.
The inhabitants would gladly have fled and chosen some
larger valley for their dwelling, but no neighboring par-
ish would receive or give up any ground to them. They
were obliged to remain beneath the menacing overhanging rocks. Every evening a few tolls of the bell remind
them of the terrors of the past, and warn them of the
fate that may perhaps overtake them during the night.

Numbers of fallen rocks, which are to be seen in the
middle of the fields, have a terrible legend attached to
them, but some few others are also shown to us which
have missed their prey. One of those enormous overhanging blocks, and whose base was rooted in the ground
on every side, rises up by the side of the road. While
admiring its superb proportions, its mighty mass, the
fineness of its grain, I could not restrain a kind of dread.
A small footpath, diverging from the road, led straight
to the foot of a formidable stone. Close to it some re-

"THE INHABITANTS COME TO CONTEMPLATE THE DISASTER."

mains of earthenware and coal were heaped up at its base, a garden paling stopped abruptly at the rock, and borders of vegetables, half overgrown by weeds, surrounded one whole side of the enormous mass.

Who had selected this strange spot for his garden and so soon abandoned it? I understood by degrees. The footpath, the accumulation of coal, the garden, had but lately belonged to a little house, now crushed beneath the rock. During the night of the downfall a man, as I learned later, was sleeping alone in that house. Starting up out of his sleep, he heard the noise of the stone falling from crag to crag down the mountain's side, and, seized with terror, he threw himself out of the window, to seek shelter behind the steep bank of the torrent. Hardly had he rushed out of his dwelling before the enormous projectile fell upon the cottage, burying it some yards deep in the ground beneath. After his fortunate escape, the brave man rebuilt his cabin; he set it up confidently at the foot of another rock which had fallen from the formidable wall.

In many mountain valleys the defiles where torrents or foot-tracks with difficulty force their way are formed by the downfall of stones called *clapiers, lapiaz,* or chaos. There is nothing more curious than the confusion of these masses mixed up in an endless labyrinth. Up above, on the side of the mountain, the color and shape of the rocks still enable us to distinguish the spot where the downfall began; but with amazement we ask ourselves how a place of such apparently small dimensions could discharge a similar deluge of stones into the valley. In the midst of these strange formidable blocks, the traveller might believe himself to be in a world in which noth-

ing reminded him of the known planet, of the smooth
or gently undulated surface. Rocks resembling fantastic monuments rise up here and there; they resemble
towers, obelisks, crenellated archways, shafts of columns,
tombs turned upside-down or standing erect. One single boulder, forming a bridge, conceals the torrent; we
see the waters rush in and disappear beneath the enormous arcade, and we even cease to hear its voice. Amid
these monstrous edifices gigantic forms appear, like those
of the fossilized animals whose disconnected bones are
sometimes found in the earth's strata. Mammoths, mas-
todons, giant turtles, winged crocodiles—all these chimerical beings swarm in the terrible chaos. Thousands of
these stones are piled up in the defile, and yet one single
specimen is of sufficient dimensions to serve as a quarry,
and to supply building materials for whole villages.

These *clapiers*, which I behold with such astonishment, and amid which I only venture hesitatingly, are
certainly trifles compared with some mountain landslips,
whose débris covers a great extent of country. There are
mountainous masses whose peaks are composed of compact heavy rocks resting upon friable beds, easily washed
away by water. In these masses the downfall of stones
is a normal phenomenon, as would be avalanches and
rain. The people are always looking up at the summits,
to see if the slip is being prepared. In a region not very
remote, and called the Country of Ruins, are two mountains which, according to the tales of the inhabitants,
had formerly been engaged in conflict together. The
two stone giants, becoming animate, are said to have
armed themselves with their own rocks, to ruin and demolish one another. They did not succeed, for they are

both still left standing; but one can imagine the prodigious heaps of rocks which, since that battle, have strewn the plains for a great distance.

Sometimes, despite his weakness, man has essayed to imitate the mountains, doing so in order to crush other men like himself. It was especially in the defiles, in places where the gorge is narrow and commanded by steep escarpments, that the mountaineers assembled to roll blocks of stone upon their enemies' heads. Thus the Basques, hidden behind brushwood upon the slopes of the mountain of Altabiscar, awaited the French army belonging to the Paladin Roland, who was to penetrate into the narrow pass of Roncesvalles. When the columns of foreign soldiers, like a long serpent gliding into a crevice in a wall, had filled the defile, a cry was heard and a hailstorm of rocks was poured down upon the crowd moving below. The stream in the valley was swollen with the blood flowing from the crushed bodies, like wine from a press; it swept away the human corpses and bruised limbs as it swept away stones in times of tempest. All the Frankish warriors perished, mixed up together in a bleeding mass. The spot where the Paladin Roland died with his companions is still shown at the foot of Altabiscar; but the stones beneath which his army was crushed have long since disappeared under a carpet of heather and furze.

The results of our small human labors are trifles compared with the natural downfall caused by the action of the weather, or in consequence of internal upheavals of the mountains. Even after long centuries, the great avalanches of stones present such a scene of confusion as to leave an impression of horror and fright on our minds.

But when nature has ended by repairing the disaster, the most beautiful spots in the mountains are precisely those where the escarpments have shaken themselves so violently as to scatter the rocks to their very base. During the course of ages the waters have done their work; they have brought clay, tenuous sand, to rebuild their beds and to form a layer of vegetable mould on their shores. The torrents have by degrees cleared their course by arranging or displacing the stones which were in their way; this monster species of pavement, formed by the smallest rocks, covered itself anew with turf and became changed into a pasture full of mounds and bristling with crags; the great rocks have clothed themselves with moss, while here and there they are grouped in picturesque miniature mountains; clumps of trees grow beside each rocky projection, and spread the most charming groups over a country which was already so lovely. Like man's countenance, the face of nature changes its physiognomy; a frown is succeeded by a smile.

Chapter VIII.

CLOUDS.

Upon the vast globe, the mountain, **lofty** as it appears, is but a single rugosity, smaller **in proportion** than would be a wart upon an elephant's body; **it is a speck, a grain of sand.** And yet that projection, **so diminutive** when compared with the great earth, bathes its **sides** and crests in aërial regions very different from those of the plains which serve as the people's dwelling-place. The pedestrian who, in the space of a few hours, ascends from the foot of the rocks to their summit in reality makes a much greater **voyage, one much more fertile** in contrasts, than if he spent years **in going round the world,** across **seas** and the lower regions of continents.

It is the air which weighs in **heavy masses** upon the ocean and countries **lying at a trifling** elevation above the level of the sea, **and in the heights** becomes rarefied, growing lighter and **lighter.** Upon the earth hundreds, and even thousands, of mountains **raise their crests in an** atmosphere whose molecules are **twice as scattered as** those in **the air** of the lower regions. **Phenomena of** light, heat, **climate, vegetation,** all **are changed** up yonder; the air, much rarer, easily allows the rays of heat to pass, whether descending **from** the sun or rising from the earth. When the orb shines in a clear sky, the **tempera-**

4

ture rapidly rises upon the higher slopes; but the moment that it hides itself, the elevated portions of the
mountain immediately become colder; radiation soon
causes them to lose the heat they had received. Cold,
too, almost always reigns in the altitudes: in our mountains it averages one degree colder in every vertical space
of two hundred yards.

As for us, poor townspeople, who are condemned to a
tainted atmosphere, who receive into our organs an air
laden with poisons which has already been breathed by
multitudes of other lungs, what astonishes us and glad-
dens us most when we wander about these high peaks is
the marvellous purity of the air. We breathe with delight, we drink in the breeze blowing around us, we allow
ourselves to become intoxicated with it. For us it is the
ambrosia talked of by ancient mythologies. Far, far
away at our feet in the plain lies extended a foggy,
dingy spot whereon our eyes can discern nothing. It is
the great city. And we think with disgust of the years
during which we have been obliged to live beneath that
sheet of smoke, dust, and impure breath.

What a contrast between that view of the plains and
the aspect of the mountain when the summit is free from
mist and we can contemplate it from afar, beyond the
heavy atmosphere weighing upon the lower regions! The
sight is beautiful, especially when the rain has caused
the floating particles of dust to fall to the ground and
the air has, so to say, grown young again. The outline
of the rocks and snow stands out clearly from the blue
of the sky; despite the enormous distance, the mountain,
blue itself as the aerial depths, is portrayed sharply
against the sky, with all its reliefs of ridges and peaks;

we can distinguish the dales, ravines, precipices; sometimes even in a black speck moving slowly over the snow we can, with the aid of a telescope, recognize a friend climbing up the peak. Of an evening after the sun has gone to rest, the pyramid displays itself at once in all the purity and splendor of its beauty. The rest of the world lies in shadow, gray twilight veils the horizon of the plains; the entrance to the valleys has already become blackened by night. But yonder, up above, all is light and joyousness. The snow, which still faces the sun, reflects its rosy rays; it **glistens, and** their brightness appears all the more vivid that the shadow, which is slowly rising, successively takes possession of the slopes **and** covers them as if with some black material. Finally, the peak alone is high enough to perceive the sun beyond the bend of the earth: it is illuminated as if it were a spark; it might be taken for one of those huge diamonds which, according to the Hindoo legends, flashed at the summit of the divine mountains. But suddenly **the** flame has disappeared, it has vanished into space. Yet we do not cease to look; the sun's reflection is succeeded by the empurpled mists on the horizon. The mountain becomes illuminated once more, but with a softer brilliancy. The hard rock no longer appears to exist beneath its apparel of rays; only a mirage remains, an aerial light; we might imagine the splendid mountain to have been detached from the earth and to be floating in the pure skies.

Thus the rarity of the air in the upper regions contributes to the beauty of the peaks by preventing the impurities of the lower atmosphere reaching the summits; but it also compels the invisible vapors rising from the sea and plains to become condensed and to attach

themselves to the **clouds, to** the sides of the mountain.
Ordinarily the vaporized water, suspended in the lower
zones of the air, is not found in sufficiently large quantities immediately to change into cloudlets and fall down
again as rain; the atmosphere in which it floats preserves
it in a state of invisible gas. But the layer of air ascending to the sky, carrying away **its** vapors, will gradually
become colder, and its water, condensed into distinct molecules, will soon reveal itself. **It** is first an almost imperceptible cloudlet, a white flake in the blue sky; but other
flakes are added to this one: now it is **a veil through**
whose rents our glances can pierce into the depths **of**
space; at last it becomes a dense mass, stretching itself
out as curtains, or piling itself up into pyramids. These
are the clouds which rise **upon** the horizon in the form
of real **mountains. Their crests and** domes, their snow,
their resplendent **ice, their shadowy** ravines, their precipices—the whole picture is displayed with perfect preci-
sion. Only the vapor mountains are floating and fugitive; one current of air has formed, another current can
rend and dissolve, them. Their duration is hardly one
of hours, while that of mountains of stones lasts for millions of years; but is the difference in reality so great?
Relatively to the world's existence, clouds and mountains
are equally the phenomena of a day. Minutes and centuries become confounded, when they are ingulfed in the
abyss of time.

Clouds **are** particularly fond of gathering round the
rocks which rise up **in the** open sky. They are attracted to the stone by an electricity the very opposite of
their own; the storms pursued into space by the wind,
dash **up** against the sides of mountains, great barriers

placed athwart their course. Others, again, invisible in the tepid **air, do not** reveal themselves until they come **in** contact with the cold stones or snow; it is the mountain that condenses the vapors and drives them out of the air, so to say. How many times, while contemplating the peak or some prominent cliff, have I seen the down of growing clouds accumulate around the frozen point! Smoke arises similar to that which ascends from a crater; soon every peak is enveloped in it, and the mountain ends by being encircled with a turban **of clouds** which **it** has woven for itself in the transparent atmosphere. Invisible **hands,** it seems, **work** at the formation of storms and the downfall of rain. When the denizens of plains see the mountain disappear in a mass of clouds, they understand, from the manner in which the giant decks his head, what sort of festival he is preparing for them. When two blasts of air chance to meet at this point, the one scorching, the other cold, the cloud thus formed suddenly raises itself up and whirls round in the sky: the mountain is a volcano, and **the** vapor escapes from it incessantly, as if in fury, to go and coil itself up again far away in the sky in an immense curve.

Detached clouds scatter themselves freely in the sky; they meet again, comb or ravel themselves out in the wind, extend or fly away, and ascend until they reach **the** upper atmosphere, far away above the highest peaks of the world. The diversity of their forms is much greater than that of those clouds which encircle the summits of the mountain. Nevertheless, these, too, present an equally singular mobility of appearance. **At** one time they are isolated clouds, displaced by great

patches of cold air; then they may be seen winding like
a serpent, as they creep through the ravines or pursue
their course along the ridges, hanging like fringes on
the sharp rocks. At another time they are great shadows concealing the whole of a mountain slope at once;
through their dense mass, which increases or diminishes,
moves away or is torn up, we can from time to time distinguish the well-known peak, all the more superb in
appearance, in proportion as it seems to live and move
among the revolving vapors. At other times the aerial
layers, superposed and of different temperature, are as
perfectly horizontal and distinct as geological strata;
the clouds which we see spring up there are of an analogous form; they are disposed in regular and parallel
belts, here hiding forests, there pastures, snow and rocks,
or semi-veiling them as if with a transparent scarf.
Sometimes again the peaks, the higher slopes, the whole
of the lofty mountain is lost in the heavy mass of
clouds, as if it were a gray or black sky that is lowered
to the earth; the mountain retreats or approaches us,
according to the play of the vapors as they diminish or
become intensified. Suddenly all disappears from base
to summit; the mountain is entirely lost in the fog;
then the storm comes down from the peaks, it lashes the
sea of heavy vapors, and we see the giant appear once
more, "gloomy, sorrowful, amid the eternal flight of the
clouds."

"WE SEE THE GIANT APPEAR ONCE MORE."

CHAPTER IX.

FOGS AND STORMS.

WE find ourselves in a new world, both fantastic and formidable, when we wander about the mountain in the midst of a mist. Even when following a well-worn foot-track upon easy slopes, we feel a certain dread on beholding the surrounding forms, whose uncertain outlines seem to oscillate in the fog, which one moment grows dense and the next becomes a little lighter.

It is necessary to know nature very well not to feel at all uneasy when we find ourselves taken captive by a fog; the least object assumes immense, infinite proportions. Something vague and black appears to be advancing upon us as if to seize us. Is it a branch or even a tree? It is but a tuft of grass. A circle of ropes bars your way; it is a simple spider's web! One day when the fog was not quite so dense and the sun's rays, transmitted through the mists, shed an indistinct light, I stopped, filled with amazement and admiration, on beholding a gigantic tree twisting its arms about like an athlete at the summit of a peak. Never had I had the good-fortune to see a stronger tree or one better situated for doing heroic battle with the tempest. I contemplated it for a long time; but by degrees I saw it apparently approaching me, and at the same time be-

4*

coming smaller. When the triumphant sun had dispersed the mist, the superb trunk proved to be nothing but a poor little tree, growing in the fissure of a neighboring rock.

The traveller who is lost, has gone astray in the fog, amid precipices and torrents, finds himself in a truly terrible position : danger or death meets him on every side. He must walk, and walk quickly, in order as fast as possible to reach the level ground of the valley or the gentle slopes of the pastures, and find some safety-bringing footpath; but, in the uncertain light, nothing serves as a guide, and everything appears to be an obstacle. On one side the ground recedes; he imagines himself to be on the edge of a precipice. On the other a rock rises up, its walls appear to be inaccessible. In order to avoid the abyss, he tries to scale the abrupt sides of the rock; he places his foot upon some uneven portion of the stone and jumps from point to point; soon he seems to be suspended in mid-air between heaven and earth. At last he reaches the ridge, but behind the first crag, see, another rises up with undecided and shifting outlines. The trees, the shrubs, growing upon the escarpments, dart their branches out into the mist in a menacing fashion; sometimes even nothing can be seen but a black mass winding its serpent-like way in the gray shadow: it is a branch whose trunk remains invisible. The wanderer's face is dripping with fine rain ; the tufts of grass, the heather, are so many reservoirs of frozen water, in which he gets quite as wet as if he were crossing through a lake. His limbs become stiff, his steps uncertain; he runs the risk of slipping upon the grass or damp rock, and of rolling down the precipice. Terrible noises ascend from below and seem to foretell a fatal end; he hears the fall of stones rolling down, of rain-laden branches creaking on their stems, the dull thunder of the cascade and the solemn breaking of the waves upon the shores of the lake. With horror he sees the fog become charged with the darkness of twilight, and he thinks of the terrible alternative of death by the uprooting of rocks or by being frozen in the cold.

In many climates, the impression of astonishment, even of horror, which the mountains leave **upon** our minds is owing to the fact of their being perpetually surrounded with mist. Such a mountain in Scotland or Norway appears formidable, whereas in reality it is much less high than many other peaks in the world. We have often seen them veiled in vapors, then partially revealed and hidden once more, travelling, so to say, into the centre of the sky, appearing to retreat that they may suddenly approach us again; growing lower when the sun clearly lights up their **outlines, then, again,** increasing when they become fringed with mists. All these changing aspects, these slow or rapid transformations, of the mountain make it vaguely resemble a prodigious giant waving his **head** above the clouds. Very different from the immovable summits, with their regular outlines, which are bathed in the pure light of Egypt's sky are those mountains sung by the poet Ossian: **they** look at you; they sometimes smile, sometimes frown, but they live in your life, they feel with you; at least so we believe, and the poet who sings them invests them with a human soul.

Beautiful on account of the vapors encircling it, when

seen from below through a pure atmosphere, the mountain is not the less so for him who contemplates it from
above, especially of a morning when the peak itself is
plunged into the sky, and its base is surrounded by a sea
of clouds. It is, indeed, a veritable ocean which extends
on every side as far as we can see. The white billows
of mist roll away upon the surface of these waters, not
with the regularity of liquid waves, but in a majestic
disorder in which our gaze loses itself. Here we see
them puffed out, swollen into towers of smoke, then dis-
perse in snow-like flakes, disappearing into space. Yonder, on the contrary, they are hollowed out into valleys
filled with shadows. In other parts it is one continued
evolution, a movement of waves pursuing and carrying
one another away in curiously contorted rings. Sometimes the sheet of vapors is tolerably smooth; the level
of the waves of mist remains at an almost uniform elevation all round the circumference of the rocks which
jut out in points; in many places the summits of isolated little hills rise up above the fog like islands or
reefs. At other times the dusky ocean divides itself
into distinct seas, here and there allowing the bottoms
of the valleys to be seen, like a lower world possessing
none of the soft serenity of the peaks. The sun obliquely lights up all the volutes of mist soaring above
the great sea, the roseate, purple, golden tints, mingled
with the pure white, impart infinite variety to the aspect
of the floating expanse. The shadow of the mountains
is projected far away upon the vapors, and changes incessantly with the course of the sun. In astonishment
the spectator beholds his own shadow reproduced upon
the sheet of vapor, and sometimes with a giant's propor-

tions. He might believe that he saw a **spectral** monster, which he causes to move at his will, as he bends, walks, stirs his arms.

Certain mountains rising from the bosom of the Blue Sea of the trade-winds are almost always encircled half-way up by a robe of mist, which almost invariably conceals the picture of the great azure plain from the traveller who has reached the peak; but around the summit, on whose pastures I am wandering, the sheets of vapor rise and descend, change and melt away, as if by chance; they are phenomena which possess no permanent peculiarities. After hours or days of obscurity, the sun **ends** in piercing the mass of fog, **rends** it asunder, scatters it in fragments, vaporizes them in the air, and soon the earth beneath, which found itself deprived of the soft radiance, becomes illuminated afresh by the quickening light. But it also happens that the fogs become denser, gather in thick and whirling clouds. These attract, then repel one another; electricity accumulates in the increasing vapors; a storm bursts, and the lower world is lost beneath the tumult of the tempest.

Once let loose, the storm does not always rise to the top of the heights which command it; it frequently remains in the lower zones of the atmosphere wherein it arises, and the spectator, seated tranquilly upon the dry turf of the upper, illuminated pastures, can see the hostile clouds come into collision, and drown everything in fury. It is both a magnificent and terrible scene. Lurid light escapes from these seething masses; copper-colored reflections, violet tints, impart to the heaped-up vapors the appearance of an immense furnace of fusing metal; the earth might have opened, allowing an ocean of lava to stream out of its bosom. The lightning flashing from cloud to cloud, in the depths of chaos, vibrates like serpents of fire. The rending of the air, reverberated by the mountain's echoes, is prolonged in endless rumblings; every rock seems simultaneously to send forth its thunder. At the same time, we hear a dull sound, ascending from the lower country through the whirling clouds. It is the downpour of rain or hail; it is the noise of trees crashing, of rocks splitting, of avalanches of stones rolling down, of torrents swelling and roaring, as they destroy their banks; but all these various noises become confused as they ascend towards the serene calm mountain. There they are but a plaint, a sigh, rising from the plain wherein man dwells.

One day, when sitting upon a tranquil peak, in the quiet of the skies, I saw a storm contort itself in fury at the foot of the mountain; I could not resist that summons which seemed to reach me from the world of humankind. I descended to bury myself in the black mass of revolving vapors; I plunged, so to say, into the midst of the thunder, beneath a sheet of lightning in the turbulence of the rain and hail. Descending by a footpath transformed into a rivulet, I leaped from stone to stone. Excited by the fury of the elements, by the bursting of the thunder-claps, by the rushing of the waters, the roar of shaken trees, I ran along in frenzied delight. When I reached the cabin in which I found a fire, bread, dry clothes, all the sweets of the mountaineer's kindly hospitality, I almost regretted the stirring ecstasy which I had so lately enjoyed outside. I felt that up above, in the wind and rain, I had taken part in the tempest, and that for a few hours my conscious individuality had been mixed up with the blind elements.

Chapter X.

SNOW.

" White, dazzling, snowy," such is almost always the original meaning of all the names given to the high mountains by the people who have succeeded one another at their base. When raising their eyes to the summits, they perceive, above the clouds, the sparkling whiteness of snow and ice; and their admiration is all the greater that the lower countries, with the uniform brown tint of their soil, present so striking a contrast to the white peaks. It is especially in summer, when the scorching dust rises from the roads, and the tired travellers stop beneath the shade, that they love to carry their gaze up to the frozen masses, resplendent as slabs of silver in the solar rays. At night a soft reflection, like that of a distant world, reveals the snow lying high upon the mountain.

The middle slopes, the lower points, are frequently covered with beds of snow. Even towards the end of summer, when the torrents have carried away into the plains the melted water of the avalanches, when the trees have shaken off the burden of whiteness which had bowed down their branches, and even the lowly mosses, while warming the surrounding parts, have freed themselves from the flakes enveloping them, a sudden chilling

of the atmosphere transforms the mountain's vapors into
crystals.   On the preceding evening all the lower chains
of the mountains and the alpine pastures had been perfectly free from hoar-frost; the brown or yellow color of
the bare rocks, the green of the forests and grass, the
purple of the heather, were all distinctly visible.

In the morning, on awaking, the white robe of snow
had covered everything, down to the farthest points.
Yet this garment of snow, this white mantle of which
the poets talk, is pierced, rent in a thousand places. The
peaks of the mountain emerge from this wrap, and the
sombre shadows of the rocks, contrasting with the whiteness, throw into relief the design of the escarpments
with all the greater distinctness. The flakes have accumulated in thick drifts in the deep ravines; on the sudden slopes they have lightly broidered the fissures, like
a delicate lace veil; on the abrupt declivities they only
show themselves here and there in brilliant spots. Every
dip in the mountain is marked out from afar in its true
form by the brilliant mould of snow which fills it; every
jutting rock reveals its protuberance and irregularities
of surface by the snowy couches of various depths, alter-
nating with the nakedness of the rock. Where the latter is formed of regular strata, the snow draws the lines
of division in the neatest possible manner. It rests upon
the cornices and detaches itself from the sides of the
landslips. Across every accident of the ground, whether
protruding or receding, we see the lines of strata contin-.
ued with surprising regularity over an extent of several
miles; they look like terraces superposed by the hand of
some giant architect.

All the same, this transient summer snow, enveloping

the mountain like a veil, and which, far from concealing its form, on the contrary reveals it in its smallest details, is, so to say, the coquetry of nature. It soon disappears from the lower hills and nearest mountains; each day the sun's rays force the limits to rise a little higher towards the summits; in fine weather even our glances can from hour to hour follow the progress of the dissolution. Each ravine, half-way up, intersecting the sides of the mountains, presents one slope upon which the midday sun freely shines, already divested of the snow, and another of dazzling whiteness, which is turned towards the horizon of the north. Then, in time, that declivity also frees its turf and pastures; nothing more remains of the summer fall of snow, but a small number of pools gradually contracting, and of traces of the miniature avalanches which filled the crevices of the gorges. These puddles mix in among the earth and boulders, and the streamlet passing by carries away drop by drop the muddy débris.

This snow, lasting a few days, is charming to behold. We love to follow with our glance the changing ornamentation; indeed, it hardly shows itself save to disappear immediately. In order to contemplate snow under its true aspect, and to understand it in its work as one of nature's agents, we should see it in winter during the severe cold season. Then all is covered with enormous layers of water crystallized into spikes and flakes; the mountain, its lower ridge, and the hills at its base no longer display themselves in their true form.

The dense mass concealing them obliterates their design, and imparts new outlines to them. In the place of points jutting out, indentations, jagged lines cut in

their outlines, the mountain's slopes now sweep down in
charming undulations, in boldly designed but yet sinuous form.   Just as water, in accordance with the laws of
gravity, finds its level, enabling it to spread out on a horizontal surface, so does the snow, obeying its own laws,
deposit itself in layers on the rounded knolls.   The wind,
driving it up as it circles round, first obliges it to fill
up the hollows, then soften all the angles, and spread its
cover over every crag; to the stern, rugged, wild mountain, a second has succeeded, with clear, softened outlines
and majestic brow.   But, in spite of the suave softness
of its lines, the giant is none the less formidable in appearance.   Escarpments, perpendicular rocks upon which
the snow cannot lie, rise up above immense slopes of
dazzling whiteness, and by contrast their walls appear
quite black.   We feel overcome with alarm at the sight
of these prodigious walls **standing** out above the snow
like cliffs of coal on the shores of a polar sea.

By this transformation the plains, even more than the
protuberances of the mountains, have altered their aspect.   The snow, falling on every side, has filled up the
cavities, levelled the hollows, caused all slighter accidents
of the ground to disappear.   Torrents, cascades, **have**
been covered up; everything is frozen, everything rests
beneath the vast winding-sheet.   Even the lakes are buried; the ice on their surface bears enormous beds of
snow, and frequently it **becomes** impossible to know
where the basins are situated; a fissure may permit us
to see the surface of the lake lying tranquil, black, void
of any reflections, at the bottom of a gulf: it looks like
a well, a fathomless abyss.

Below the great summits and upper amphitheatres,

where the snow is piled up in mounds high as houses, the pine forests stand out here and there, but only one half of them is visible. Upon each of their extended branches the trees bear as heavy a load as they can support without breaking; the confusion of boughs together forms arches upon which the accumulation of snowy crystals is grouped in unequal cupolas; some rebellious trunks alone escape from the icy prison, and shoot their dark-green, almost black, arrows into the free air, each one bearing at its extremity a heavy lump of **snow**. When the wind whistles through these stems, fragments of the frozen snow fall down with a metallic sound; a general movement of vibration stirs the hidden forest and the glistening roof covering it: sometimes a rupture takes place, an avalanche rolls down inside, a gaping chasm is left, until a fresh storm has masked it beneath a bridge of snow. What would be the fate of the traveller who had lost his way in the winter in such a forest— one through which he could walk where he liked in the summer, along the short grass, beneath the shade of the mighty trees? At each step he is liable to tumble into an abyss, to be suffocated beneath the fallen snow.

The village houses in **the** valley below seem to **be** more difficult to discern than the forests and clumps of trees. The roofs, entirely covered with a bed of snow, beneath them the bending woodwork, become mixed up with the surrounding fields of whiteness; only a delicate bluish smoke reminds us that beneath this white shroud men live and work. Some walls, a distant steeple, break the monotony of the valley; besides, in that part the snow has been more storm-driven than where it is far from human habitations: the wind, whirling round the dwellings, has raised it up into hillocks and barricades on the one side; the other it has swept almost perfectly clean. A certain disorder in nature indicates the proximity of man; but there, as elsewhere, endless peace prevails; rarely does a sound come to disturb the silence of death reigning over mountain and valley.

Yet sometimes it is necessary that man and the other inhabitants of the mountains should leave their dens and disturb nature's great repose. Only the marmot, hidden in its hole under the deep snow, can sleep away the long months of winter, and, apparently in a dead state, await spring's coming to restore freedom to the brooks, the grass, and flowers. The chamois, less fortunate, driven from the lofty heights by the snow, is obliged to wander in the neighborhood of forests, seeking refuge among the crowded trees, consuming their bark and leaves. Man, on his part, must leave his home to exchange some articles of produce, buy provisions, fulfil family or friendly engagements. Then it is necessary to sweep away mounds of snow accumulated before his door, and laboriously make himself a pathway. Once, from a chalet built upon a high promontory, I saw some of these almost imperceptible beings, these black human ants, walking slowly along a sort of track between two walls of snow. Never had man appeared so insignificant. In the midst of the vast extent of whiteness, these pedestrians appeared absurdly chimerical. I asked myself how a race composed of such pygmies had been able to accomplish all the great historical deeds, and, step by step, to carry out that which to-day we term civilization, the promise of a future state of well-being and liberty.

Yet even in the midst of these formidable winter

snows man has been able to cause his intelligence and
audacity to triumph by means of those commercial roads
which permit him freely to despatch his merchandise
and to travel in almost all weathers. The chamois has
ceased to roam about the summits, and numbers of birds,
flying above the peaks in summer, have prudently descended into the milder regions of the plains. But man
continues to traverse those roads, ascending from gorge
to gorge, from chain to chain, until they reach a gap in
the crest and again descend the other slope. During
the fine season, when the glad torrents bound in cascades
by the roadside, even the carriages drawn by horses,
with their tinkling bells, can without difficulty scale
the incline made at such expense up the escarpments.
When the road is covered with snow, it is necessary to
change the means of conveyance: carts and carriages
are replaced by sleighs that glide lightly over the heaped-
up flakes. The ascent of the mountains is no less rapid
than in the hottest days of summer; as to the descent, it
is accomplished at a dizzy pace.

It is in travelling thus in a sleigh over the necks of
the mountains that we can become thoroughly acquainted with deep snow. The light wooden conveyance glides
noiselessly along; we no longer feel the jolting of the
iron upon the resisting ground, and we might imagine
ourselves to be travelling into space, as if borne away by
some spirit. At one moment we round the bend of a
ravine, the next the point of some crag; we pass from
the bottom of a chasm to the edge of a precipice, and in
all these various forms, which pass successively before
our gaze, the mountain preserves its uniform whiteness.
If the sun lights up the snowy surface, we see it glisten-

ing with countless diamonds; should the sky be gray
and low, the elements seem to merge into one another;
fragments of clouds, of snowy hillocks, can no longer be
distinguished from each other: we might imagine ourselves to be floating in infinite space; we cease to belong
to the earth.

And how much more we enter into the land of dreams
when, after having attained the culminating point of the
pass, we once again descend the opposite slope, carried
round turning after turning with alarming rapidity! At
the caravan's departure, when the last sleigh starts the
first has already disappeared behind a projection in the
gulf. We see it, then it disappears again; we perceive
it once more, to be lost anew. We plunge into a dizzy
abyss wherein heaps of snow as big as small hills are
rolling down. An avalanche ourselves, we slide down
other avalanches, and we see amphitheatres, ravines,
crags, defiling at our side as if they were drawn along
by a tempest; even the summits themselves, soaring to
the horizon, seem to be swept along in a fantastic whirl-
wind, in a species of infernal gallop. And when, at the
end of the unbridled race, we arrive at the foot of the
mountain in the plains, already cleared from the snow or
slightly powdered over with it, when we breathe another
atmosphere and behold a new nature in another climate,
we ask ourselves if we have not really been the play-
thing of some hallucination, if we have indeed crossed
that deep snow above the region of clouds and tempests?

But on those days during which a storm lasts, the
transit is perilous enough for a traveller to remember it,
to retain a very distinct recollection of all his adventures.
The hurricane incessantly drives up whirlwinds of snow

"THERE IS THE ABYSS."

which hide the road and modify its form, reducing the
slopes and filling up the road, rough enough already.
The horses, so sure-footed on solid ground, have sometimes to cross through heaps of soft, deep drifts; while
the one sinks into them up to his chest, another stumbles
over a piled-up mound. The tempest whistling round
their ears, the flakes blowing into their eyes and nostrils,
the brutal oaths of the drivers, irritate and threaten to
madden them. The sleigh jolts up the narrow way, now
bending towards the mountain wall, now towards the
precipice, for there is the abyss; we graze its edges, follow it afar to an immense distance, as if in falling we
must go down into another world. The coachman has
put down his whip; he holds nothing but a knife in his
hand now, ready to cut the traces if the horses, bewildered
with fear or slipping down a snowy slope, should suddenly roll over the precipice.

Terrible is the unhappy pedestrian's position when,
slowly crossing the snow, he is all at once overtaken by
a storm. The people in the plains composedly contemplate the weather. The mountain-peak, lashed by the
wind, seems to smoke like a crater; the countless frozen
molecules tossed up by the tempest gather in the clouds
whirling above the summits. The contours of the ridges,
blurred by this mist of circling snow, appear less regular—they look as if they were floating in space; even
the mountain seems to oscillate on its enormous base.
And what becomes of the poor traveller amid this dizzy
whirl of the tempest as it whistles around the high
peaks? The spicules of ice, hurled against him like arrows, beat his face and threaten to blind him; they even
penetrate his clothes; he can hardly defend himself

against them, wrapped as he is in his thick cloak. When, making a false step or following a wrong track, he leaves the footpath for one moment, he is almost inevitably lost. He walks along by chance, falling from one drift into another. Sometimes he sinks half-way up into a hole of soft snow; he remains in it some time, as if awaiting his death in the grave that opens out beneath him; then, in despair, he raises himself up again and recommences his rough way through the clouds of crystals driven into his face by the wind. The squalls alternately approach and retreat from the horizon. At one moment he sees nothing around him but the white smoke of the circling flakes; at another, on his right or left, he can distinguish a tranquil peak shaking off the clouds and looking at him, "without hatred and without love," indifferent to his despair; in it, at least, he sees a sort of landmark, allowing him to resume his way with some return of hope. But in vain; blinded, maddened, stiffened with the cold, he ends by losing all power of volition; he turns round and round, and struggles aimlessly on. At last he falls into some chasm, gazes in stupor at the whirling storm as it sweeps over him, and by degrees allows sleep, the precursor of death, to overcome him. In a few months, when the snow shall have been melted by the heat and swept away by avalanches, some sheepdog will find the body, and by his terrified barking summon his master.

Formerly any human remains found in the mountain had to rest forever in the place where the shepherd discovered them. Rocks were piled up above the corpse, and every passer-by was bound to add his stone to the increasing cairn. Even nowadays any mountaineer passing one of these ancient tombs never fails to pick up his stone wherewith to enlarge the pile. The dead person has long since been forgotten—perhaps his identity was never even known; but from century to century the passer-by never ceases to render homage to him, hoping to appease his manes.

Chapter XI.

AVALANCHES.

At last the long winter and its redoubtable storms
have been succeeded by sweet spring-time, with its rains,
its mild winds, its vivifying warmth. Everything grows
young again; the mountain as well as the plain assumes
a new aspect.   It shakes off its mantle of snow; its forests, turf, cascades, and lakes appear once more beneath
the sun's rays.

In the valley, man was the first to rid himself of the
accumulated snow which inconvenienced him. He has
swept the threshold of his door, mended his roads, freed
his roofs and garden, and then waits for the sun to do
the rest.   The *soulanes*, or slopes, well exposed to the
southern rays, begin to cast off the white winding-sheet
that shrouds them ; here and there the rock, earth, or turf
reappears through the snowy bed.   These black patches increase by degrees; they resemble groups of islands
incessantly growing bigger, and ending by joining one
another: the white spots diminish in number and size;
they melt, and seem gradually to reascend the mountain
slope.   The forest trees, awaking from their torpor, begin to put on their spring garb; assisted by the little
birds, fluttering from branch to branch, they shake off
the burden they bear of hoar-frost and snow, and freely
bathe their new shoots in the milder atmosphere.

The torrents, too, regain their animation. Beneath the protecting bed of snow, the temperature of the ground has never fallen so low as at the outer surface swept by the cold winds; and, during long months of winter, small reservoirs of water, like the little drops in a diamond vessel, retain their natural state here and there beneath the ice. In the spring-time these urns, towards which flow all the tiny rills of melted snow, no longer suffice to retain the liquid mass; the frozen coverings burst, the basins overflow, and the water seeks to hollow a path out for itself beneath the snow. In every ravine, every depression of the ground, this hidden work goes on; and the torrent in the valley, fed by all these rivulets descending from above, resumes its course, which had been interrupted by the cold of the winter. At first it passes through a tunnel, beneath heaped-up snow; then, owing to the incessant progress of the thaw, it enlarges its bed and raises its vaults. The moment arrives in which the mass above cannot any longer preserve its entirety; it gives way as would the roof of a temple whose pillars were shaken. Thus leaks are opened out in the accumulated snow, filling up the bottom of the valleys; when we lean over the edge of these chasms, we can see in their depths a black object upon which a little foam is broidering ephemeral lacework. It is the water of the torrent; the dull murmur of the stones dashing against each other rises from the gloomy aperture.

This first giving-way of snow is succeeded by others more and more numerous; and soon the torrent, once again free to a great extent, has nothing left but to throw down the dams formed by the thickest and most compact snow. Some of these ramparts resist the action of the waters for weeks and months. Even on the edges of the cascades masses of snow, converted into ice and incessantly sprinkled with the water breaking forth, obstinately retain their form; it is as if they refused to dissolve. We frequently see before the busy cataract of the torrents a sort of screen formed by a solidified waterfall; it is the frozen snow which arrested the flow of the water during the winter. While remaking their beds in every valley passing along the base of the mountains, in every ravine furrowing their sides, the waters of the brooks and torrents carry away from the snow on the slopes the basement serving as its support. The action of this pressure tends to produce avalanches, and from time to time the mountain, like an animate creature, throws the snowy garment from off its shoulders. In all seasons, even in the severest portion of the winter, masses of snow, carried away by their own weight, roll from the summits and slopes; but these avalanches being merely composed of the superficial portion of the snow, they are but a trifling incident in the mountain's life. Sometimes, however, it is the entire mass of the winter covering that slips from the heights to cast itself into the valleys; the water, or melted snow, hardly able to penetrate through the still frozen surface beds, has rendered the ground slippery, thus preparing the way for the avalanche. The moment arrives when a whole field of snow is no longer attached to the slope; it gives way, and, by the great shock it imparts to that adjoining, causes it also to yield. The whole mass is simultaneously precipitated down the side of the mountain, pushing before it all the débris met with on its course—trunks of trees, stones, blocks of rock. Dragging away with it great layers of the adjacent surface, and overthrowing more distant forests, the formidable downfall at one blow sweeps away a whole side of a mountain several hundred yards in extent, and the valley becomes partially filled with it. The torrents, dashing up against the obstacle, are obliged, temporarily, to convert themselves into lakes.

Of the bulk of these avalanches, both mountaineers and travellers invariably speak with dread. And some valleys, more exposed than others, have received sinister names in the local *patois*, such as "The Valley of Horror," or "The Gorge of the Earthquake."

I know one, the most terrible of all, into which the muleteers never venture without keeping their eyes fixed upon the heights. Especially on those fine spring days, when the mild, soft atmosphere is filled with dissolved vapors, are the travellers' looks anxious and their words few. They know that the avalanche is simply waiting for a shock, for a disturbance of the air or ground, in order to set itself in motion. At these times they walk like thieves, with rapid, cautious steps; sometimes even they wrap straw round their mules' bells, so that the tinkling of the metal may not irritate the evil spirit menacing them up above. At last, when they have passed the outlet of those redoubtable ravines, where the mountain rivulets simultaneously let loose their avalanches on several sides, they can breathe in peace, and think, without personal anxiety, of their less happy predecessors, of whom they were telling such terrible tales the evening before. Frequently, while the travellers are tranquilly continuing their descent towards the plain, a sound of thunder, a prolonged roar reverberating from rock to rock, compels them suddenly to turn round; it is the fall of snow that has just taken place, and has filled the gorge through which they passed a few moments ago.

Happily the disposition and form of the slopes permit the mountaineers to recognize such dangerous localities. Thus they do not build their cabins below a declivity whereon avalanches are formed, and, in tracing out their footpaths, take care to select sheltered routes. But everything changes in nature, and one of these little houses or footpaths, which so lately had nothing to fear, ends by finding itself exposed to danger; the angle of a projection may have disappeared, the direction of the channel of the avalanche may have been slightly diverted, the protecting outskirts of a forest have given way beneath the pressure of the snow, and consequently all the mountaineers' precautions have proved futile.

In consequence of the thousands of columns of closely packed trunks, woods are one of the best barriers against the progress of these avalanches, and numbers of villages possess no other means of defence against the snow. And with what respect, what almost religious veneration, do the people regard their sacred wood! The stranger walking about their mountains admires the forest for the sake of the beauty of its trees, the contrast of its verdure with the white snow; but they, they owe to it life and repose; it is, thanks to it, that they can go tranquilly to sleep of an evening without fear of being swallowed up during the night. Full of gratitude towards the protecting forest, they have deified it. Woe be to him who touches one of its shielding trunks with his axe! "He who kills the sacred tree kills the mountaineer," says one of their proverbs.

And yet such murderers have been met with, and in

great numbers. Just as in our days, even so-called "civilized" soldiers compel the inhabitants of an oasis to submit, by hewing down their palm-trees, which are the life of the tribe, so has it often occurred that, in order to reduce the mountaineers, invaders, in the pay of some lord, or even shepherds from another valley, have cut down the trees which served the villages as a safeguard against destruction. Such were, such are still, the practices of war. Not less ferocious is greedy speculation when, by right of purchase or the chances of inheritance or conquest, a moneyed man has become the proprietor of a sacred forest; woe be to those whose fate depends upon his benevolence or caprice! Soon the wood-cutters are at work in the forest, the trunks are hewn down, thrown into the valley, sold as planks, and paid for in good sterling dollars. Thus a wide road is laid open for the avalanches. Deprived of their outwork, it may be that the inhabitants of the threatened village persist in remaining for the sake of their natal hearth: but sooner or later the peril becomes imminent; they are obliged to migrate in all haste, to carry away their precious possessions, and to leave the house a prey to the tottering snow.

Terrible chronicles of avalanches are related to night-watchers in all mountain villages, and the children listen while nestling up against their mothers' knees. What the fire-damp is to a miner is an avalanche to a mountaineer. It menaces his chalet, his barns, his cattle; it may swallow up himself. How many relatives, friends, has he known who now sleep beneath the snow! Of an evening when he passes by the place where the enormous mass ingulfed them, it seems to him that the mountain whence the avalanche was let loose looks

5*

wickedly at him, and he redoubles his pace in order to
hasten from the sinister spot. Sometimes, also, the débris
of the downfall reminds him of a comrade's unhoped-
for escape. Yonder, on one spring night, a sloping bed
of snow, higher than the tallest fir-trees and the village
tower, fell down. A group of cottages and barns lay
beneath the formidable mass. No doubt, thought the
mountaineers who had hastened up from the neighboring
hamlets—no doubt the woodwork had been demolished
and the inhabitants would be lying crushed beneath the
ruins! Yet they set bravely to work to remove the
enormous heap. They labor on for four days and four
nights, and when at last their spades reach the roof of
the first chalet they hear voices singing in answer to one
another. These are the voices of the friends whom they
imagined to be lost. Their houses had withstood the
violence of the shock, and the air which they contained
had happily been sufficient. During the people's imprisonment they had spent their time in establishing
communication from house to house, and in digging a
tunnel of egress, singing at the same time so as to en-
courage themselves over their work.

When once the protecting forests have disappeared, it
is very difficult to replace them. Trees grow slowly on
all parts of the mountains; in the channels of the avalanches they do not grow at all. It is true that by means
of engineering works the snow can be kept safely on the
high slopes, and thus the disaster of its fall into the valleys be prevented; the declivity might be hewn into
horizontal terraces upon which the beds of snow would
be obliged to rest, as upon the steps of a gigantic staircase; the trunks of trees might be replaced by rows of

iron stakes and palisades, which would prevent the slip-
ping-down of the upper masses. These attempts have
already been made successfully, but only in valleys inhabited by a rich and numerous population. Poor villagers, unless they are aided by the world at large, would
never think of thus carving afresh the exterior of the
mountain, and the avalanches continue to fall upon the
meadows by their accustomed channels. The villagers
are obliged to confine themselves to protecting their little
houses by enormous spurs of stone, breaking the force of
the slipping snow, and dividing it into two currents when
it does not descend in masses sufficiently powerful to demolish everything at one shock.

Of all the destroyers of the mountains, an avalanche is
the most energetic. It carries away with it earth and
rocky fragments as would an overflowing torrent; still
more by the gradual melting of the snow, forming its
lower strata, it so moistens the ground that the latter becomes changed into soft mud, fissured with deep crevices,
and sinking down beneath its own weight. The earth
has become fluid to a great depth; it flows along the
whole length of the slopes, drawing with it footpaths,
blocks of scattered rocks, even houses and forests. Whole
sides of mountains, rendered sodden by the snow, have
thus slipped down in one mass with their fields, their
pastures, their woods, and their inhabitants. Thus by
their heaping up, and the melting water penetrating so
slowly into the ground, flakes of snow suffice little by
little to demolish the mountains. In spring every ravine
clearly betrays this work of destruction; cascades, landslips, avalanches, snow, rocks, and water descend in confusion from the summits and make their way towards
the plain.

Chapter XII.

GLACIERS.

Even in the midst of summer, when all the snow is melted by the breath of the warm winds, enormous accumulations of ice, imprisoned in the upper valleys, still produce a local winter, appearing all the more curious from the contrast. When the sun shines with all its brilliancy, both the direct heat and that sent forth by the glaciers are felt oppressively by the traveller; it even seems to be hotter than in the valleys, owing to the dryness of the air, incessantly deprived of its humidity by the glacier's greedy surface. Birds can be heard singing close by beneath the foliage; flowers stud the grass, fruit ripens under the whortleberry leaves. And yet, side by side with this joyous world, there lies the gloomy glacier, with its gaping crevices, its collection of stones, its terrible silence, its apparent immobility. It is death by the side of life.

Nevertheless, the great frozen mass possesses its motion also: slowly, but with an invincible force, it works as do the wind, snow, rain, running water, to renew the planet's surface. Wherever glaciers have passed over, during one of the ages of the earth's existence, the aspect of the country has been transformed by their action. As do avalanches, they carry the rubbish of the crumbling mountains into the plains, not by violence, but by the patient labor of every moment.

The work of the glacier, so difficult to discover in its secret progress, although so vast in its results, commences from the summit of the mountain, on the surface of the snowy strata. Up above in the amphitheatres where the clouds of white spicules, lashed by the storm, have been collected in whirlwinds, the uniform expanse of the snow-banks does not change its aspect. From year to year, from century to century, it is always the same whiteness, pale beneath the shadow of the clouds, dazzling beneath the rays of the sun. It appears as if the snow were eternal there, and it is thus designated by the inhabitants of the plains, who from below see it shining beside the heavens. They believe that it remains forever upon the lofty peaks, and that if the wind, during storms, does lift it up, it is always allowed to fall back into the same place.

It is nothing of the sort. One portion of the snow evaporates and returns to the clouds, whence it descended. Another portion, exposed to the rays of the sun, or to the influence of a hot southern wind, is sprinkled over with tiny melted drops, trickling down the surface or penetrating the strata until, seized upon again by the cold, they become congealed into imperceptible gems. Thus, by means of the millions of molecules which melt, then freeze to melt again, and again grow solid, the mass of snow becomes insensibly transformed; at the same time, owing to the weight which carries away the melted drops for several inches, it becomes displaced, and little by little the snow, so lately fallen upon the summit of the mountain, is found to have descended the slopes.

Other snow has taken its place, and will flow again in turn by a series of fusions, without, however, having to suffer the least apparent change. It is true that they have the infinitude of ages before them; slowly they move on towards the sea, where they must one day be swallowed up. By the time that two generations of men have succeeded one another in the lower plains, one of these flakes of snow, fallen from a lofty peak, will not yet have issued from the mass of the snow.

But, slow as it may be, this flake, converted into a crystal, does not the less hold on in its course. The mass of snow, which has become homogeneous, and has already been transformed into ice, gets entangled in the mountain gorge, whither its weight draws it. Always immovable in appearance, the accumulation of ice has now become a real river flowing in a rocky bed. Upon the slopes to the right and left, the winter's snow is completely melted, and flowering plants have replaced it; a whole world of insects lives and buzzes amid the grass of the pastures; the air is soft, and man leads his flocks on to the grassy escarpments whence his glance can descend from afar upon the frozen stream. The latter, by unceasing efforts, continues its journey to the plain; it would stretch itself out as far as the level fields at the foot of the mountains—it would reach the sea itself—if the mild temperature of the lower valleys, the warmth of the winds, the rays of the sun, did not succeed in melting the foremost ice.

On its course, the solid river behaves as would a real one of running water. It has its meanderings, its eddies, its depths and shallows, its "torpids," its rapids, and its cascades. Like the water, which expands or contracts

GLACIER AND CREVASSE.

according to the form of its bed, the ice adapts itself to the dimensions of the ravine containing it. It knows exactly how to mould itself upon the rock, as well in the vast basin whose walls widen out on either side as in the defile, where the passage almost closes up. Impelled by the masses, incessantly fed by the upper snow, the glacier continues to slide upon the bottom, the incline of which is almost insensible, or else forms a succession of precipices.

But the ice, not possessing the suppleness, the fluidity, of water, accomplishes, with a somewhat barbaric awkwardness, all the movements forced upon it by the nature of the ground. It cannot, at its cataracts, fall in one level sheet as does the water current; but, according to the inequalities of the bottom and the cohesion of the ice crystals, it fractures, splits, gets cut up into blocks inclining various ways, falling over one another, becoming cemented together again in curious obelisks, towers, fantastic groups. Even in that part where the bottom of the immense groove inclines with tolerable regularity, the surface of the glacier does not in the least resemble the even surface of the water of a river. The friction of the ice against its edges does not ripple it with tiny waves similar to those of the shore, but fractures and refractures it with crevices, intersecting one another in a labyrinth of fissures.

In winter, and even when spring has already renewed the ornamentation of the lower countries, a great number of crevasses are concealed beneath thick masses of snow, extending in continued layers along the surface of the glacier; then, if the granulous snow has not been softened by the sun's heat, it is easy to walk above the

mouth of these hidden abysses. The traveller can ignore
them, as he ignores the open caves in the thickness of
the mountains. But the annual return of the summer
season by degrees melts the superficial snow. The glacier, moving on incessantly, and whose fractured mass
vibrates in one continual tremor, shakes off the snowy
mantle covering it; here and there the vaults fall in,
and in great fragments bury themselves in the depths of
the crevasses; frequently nothing remains but the narrow bridges upon which no person would venture without having tested the solidity of the snow with his foot.

It is then that it becomes dangerous to traverse many
a glacier on account of the width of its fissures, branch-
ing out to infinity. From the edges of the chasm we
sometimes see in the interior of the superposed layers of
bluish ice, which recently were snow and are separated
by blackish bands, the remains of débris fallen upon the
snow; at other times the ice, clear, homogeneous in its
whole mass, appears to be but one single crystal.

What is the depth of the well? We do not know. A
jutting crag of ice, combined with the darkness, prevents
our glance descending to the lowest rocks; yet we sometimes hear a mysterious noise ascending from the abyss:
it is the water rippling, a stone becoming loosened, a bit
of ice splitting off and falling down.

Explorers have descended these chasms to measure
their density and to study the temperature and composition of the deep ice. Sometimes they have been able to
do it without any great risk, by penetrating laterally into
the clefts, by the jutting rocks which serve as banks to
the rivers of ice. Frequently, too, they have been obliged
to be let down by means of ropes, as is the miner who

penetrates to the bosom of the earth. But for one scientific discoverer who, taking all necessary precautions,
thus explores the holes of the glaciers, how many unhappy shepherds have been ingulfed and met their death in
those chasms! Yet we know of mountaineers who, having fallen to the bottom of these crevasses, wounded,
bleeding, lost in the darkness, have preserved their courage and the resolution to see daylight once more. There
was one who followed the course of a sub-glacial stream,
and thus made a veritable journey below the enormous
vault of pieces of falling ice. After a similar excursion,
there is nothing left for the man to do but to descend
into the chasm of a crater to explore the subterranean
reservoir of lava.

We are certainly bound to award great praise to the
courageous savant who descends into the depths of the
glacier to study its channels or grooves, its air-bubbles, its
crystals; but how many things may we not contemplate
on the surface, how many charming details are we not
permitted to perceive, how many laws are not revealed
to our eyes, if we know how to look!

Really, in this apparent chaos everything is regulat-
ed by laws. Why should a fissure always be produced
in the frozen mass opposite one point of the steep
bank? Why at a certain depth below should the crevasse,
which has gradually become enlarged, again bring its
edges nearer each other and the glacier be recemented?
Why should the surface regularly bulge out in one part
to become fissured elsewhere? On seeing all these phenomena, which roughly reproduce the ripples, wavelets, and eddies on the smooth sheets of the water of
a river, we better understand the unity which, under

such an infinity of aspects, presides over everything in nature.

When, by long exploration, we have become familiar with the glacier, and we know how to account to ourselves for all the little changes which take place upon its surface, it is a delight, a joy, to roam about it on a fine summer's day. The heat of the sun has endowed it with voice and motion. Tiny veins of water, almost imperceptible at first, are formed here and there; these unite in sparkling streamlets which wind at the bottom of miniature river-beds, hollowed out by themselves, and then suddenly disappear in a fissure in the ice, giving forth a low plaint in a silvery voice. They swell or fall according to the variations of the temperature. Should a cloud pass before the sun and cool the atmosphere, they barely continue to flow; when the heat becomes greater, the superficial rivulets assume the pace of torrents; they sweep away with them sand and pebbles to be deposited in alluvions, or to form high banks and islands; then towards evening they calm down, and soon the cold of the night congeals them afresh.

Beneath the rays of heat temporarily animating the field of the glacier by melting the superficial layer, the little world of pebbles, fallen from the neighboring walls, also becomes agitated. A gravel slope, situated on the edge of a murmuring stream of water, subsides by partial downfalls and plunges into the fissures. Elsewhere, black, broken stones are scattered over the glacier; they absorb and concentrate the heat, making holes in the ice beneath them, piercing it with little cylindrical apertures. Farther off, on the contrary, vast accumulations of débris and big stones prevent the heat of the sun penetrating below; on every side the ice melts and evaporates. In the end these stones form pillars which appear to grow, to spring out of the ground like columns of marble; but each one, too weak, at last breaks beneath the weight, and all the fragments that it bore fall down with a crash, to recommence a similar evolution on the morrow. How much more charming are all these little dramas of inanimate nature when animals or plants take part in them! Attracted by the mildness of the air, the butterfly flutters on the scene, while the plant which fell down from the heights of the neighboring rocks in a landslip utilizes its short reprieve of life to take root again, and to display to the sun its last corolla. Navigators on the polar coast have seen a whole carpet of vegetation cover a high cliff composed of earth at the top and ice at the base.

Chapter XIII.

MORAINES AND TORRENTS.

All these small phenomena daily taking place appear to be a very trifling matter in the earth's history. What, indeed, is the work of a glacier during a summer's day? Its mass, moving onward with an unceasing effort, has hardly progressed one inch; two or three rocks have become detached from the walls in order to fall upon the moving field of ice; the stream, carrying away the melted water, has spread out wider in its bed; the pebbles become more numerous, and dash against each other with greater noise. Otherwise everything has preserved its customary appearance. Nowhere does nature seem to be slower in its work of perpetual renovation.

And yet these daily, momentary, trifling transformations end by bringing about immense changes in the earth's aspect, veritable geological revolutions. These pebbles, these fragments of rock, falling from the upper escarpments on to the bed of ice, become piled up, little by little, at the base of the walls as enormous ramparts of stones; they move slowly on with the frozen mass that bears them; but other débris, which has rolled down the same channels of the mountain, replaces them in the localities they have just vacated. Thus long convoys of confusedly piled-up rocks accompany the glacier

on its course; streams of stones are added to the stream
of ice descending from every ruined height, from every
cirque furrowed by avalanches.

When it has reached the outlet of the upper gorges,
situated in the regions of a milder temperature, the glacier cannot retain its crystalline condition; it thaws and
becomes water, allowing its burden of stones to drop.
All this débris rolls down in gross confusion, forming a
dam in the valley. At the extremity of many a glacier
there are positive mountains of crumbling stones on the
loosely built-up slopes. After a long course of years
abounding in snow, the mass of the glacier swells and
lengthens, until it is obliged to pick up these mountains
of stones once more and to push them a little farther
down into the valley. Later on, when under the influence of a softer temperature of winters, when the snow
is less profuse, all the lower part of the glacier will melt,
leaving bare the basin of rocks which served as its bed;
the "moraine" of boulders, delivered from the pressure
which pushed it forward, will remain isolated at a certain
distance from the glacier; behind it will be visible the
bare polished stone, rubbed smooth by the enormous
weight so lately moving over it, and here and there
covered by a reddish-hued mud, produced by the crush-
ing of the pebbles and gravel carried away. Another
moraine of heaped-up débris will be formed little by little in front of the talus of the glacier.

Thus, then, at enormous distances ahead of the valley,
for miles and tens of miles, indisputable traces of the
former action of the ice are to be seen. Whole plains,
once filled with water, have been gradually overwhelmed
with mud and pebbles pushed on before it by the glac-

ier; the protuberances of the mountains and hills, met
with in its course by the solid stream, have been worn
and polished; finally, scattered rocks and moraines have
been deposited even as far away as the slopes of mountains belonging to other groups. The origin of these
stones is easily recognized by their chemical composition,
the arrangement of their crystals or their fossils; frequently even their distinctive characters are so precise
as to enable us to point out upon the mountain itself the
elevated *cirque* whence the missing block has been detached. For how many years or centuries has the voyage lasted? Very many, no doubt, if we judge by the
big rocks which the actual glaciers carry away, and whose
progress has been measured. Among these travelling
blocks are some which scientific men have rendered
famous by their observations, and which we love to see
again as if they were friends.

These stones cast into the plains, these accumulations
of mud transported to a great distance, all these traces
left by the ancient glaciers' sojourn, permit us to imagine
what have been the great alternations of the climate, and
the immense modifications in the exterior and aspect of
the earth during the successive ages of the planet. In
that past, revealed to us by these remains, we see our
mountain and its neighbors rising up above their actual
summits. The supreme peaks passed beyond the highest
clouds, and all the vapors travelling through space deposited themselves as snow or frozen crystals upon the
slopes of the enormous mass; the pastures, the verdant
valleys, the now wooded sloping sides, were covered by a
uniform layer of ice. Then neither cascades, lakes, rivulets, nor meadows had made their appearance in the val-

ley. The immense frozen stream, not less thick than are
now the strata of the mountains, filled up all the depressions; then, on issuing from the gorges, stretched itself
far away into the plains, below hills and dales. Such, in
our forefathers' times, was the image presented to them
by the ice-laden mountain; for our sons' grandsons, in the
remote uncertainty of centuries, the scene will again be
changed. Perhaps the glacier, then completely thawed,
will be replaced by a feeble rivulet; the mountain will
have ceased to exist; a slight rise in the ground will
mark its former site; and the actual plain, turned topsy-
turvy by the alterations in its level, will have given birth
to heights gradually growing up into the skies!

And while we muse upon the history of the mountain
and its glacier, what they were, and what they will one
day become, yonder is the little torrent murmuring as it
issues from the ice, and going forth into the world to
work at the task of continually renewing the earth. The
water, rendered white or milky by the innumerable molecules of triturated rock which it bears suspended, is neither more nor less than the glacier itself suddenly transformed into a liquid state; and yet what a contrast between the solid mass with its crevices, its caves, its piles
of stones, its muddy slopes, and the water gayly bursting
forth into daylight, and babbling as it winds amid the
flowers! That sudden apparition of the stream, which
during all its upper course has moved along in darkness,
swelling as it goes by the addition of millions of little
drops falling from the clefts in the vault, is one of the
most curious spectacles in the mountain. The cavern
whence the current escapes changes its form every day
according to the falling and melting of the ice; yet ordi-

G

narily it is easy to penetrate to a certain distance inside
the grotto, and to admire its pendants, its translucent
walls, the bluish light, the changing reflections.   The
strangeness of the sight, the vague apprehension that
overcomes our spirit, leads us to imagine that we are
transported into a sacred place.   " Three times and a
thousand times blessed " those Hindoo pilgrims believe
themselves to be, who, after having reascended the Ganges as far as its source, are also permitted to penetrate
beneath the gloomy vault whence the holy river shoots
forth.

The glacial torrents bring into the plains, with great
regularity, dependent upon that of the season, the fertilizing water and the alluvial mud arising from that enormous laboratory of trituration incessantly at work beneath the glacier.   During the cold season of our tem-
perate zones, when the rains fall most frequently upon
the fields, and, instead of evaporating, find their way towards the rivers, the glacier becomes more compactly
frozen, adheres everywhere to the vault serving as its
bed, and merely allows the feeblest little rill to escape.
Sometimes even it dries up altogether; not a drop of
water descends from the mountain.   But in proportion
as the warmth returns and the glad vegetation demands
a greater quantity of water for its flowers, in proportion
as evaporation becomes more active and the level of the
rivers tends to fall, the torrents of the glaciers swell, they
are temporarily changed into rivers and furnish the necessary moisture to the thirsty fields.   Thus is established
a balance most advantageous for the prosperity of the
countries irrigated by watercourses which are partially
fed by glaciers.   When, swollen by rain, the tributary

THE TORRENT.

streams overflow, the mountain torrents bring but a small liquid stream; they, on the other hand, overflow when the other rivers are almost dry. Thanks to this law of adjustment, a certain equality is maintained in the river wherein all the divers watercourses unite.

In the general economy of the earth, the glacier, apparently motionless, always so slow and calm in its action, is a great element of organization. Rarely does it introduce any disturbance into nature. Such a thing may happen, as, for instance, when a lateral glacier, pushing a large mound of débris, or advancing alone across a stream which issued from the primary glacier, gathers together the waters flowing from it, and thus forms a constantly increasing lake. For a long time the dam resists the pressure of the liquid mass, but, after a considerable melting of the snow, a recoil of the glacier, forming a dam, or of the *déblais,* slowly produced by the water, it is quite possible that the barrier of ice and accumulated boulders may suddenly give way. Then the lake breaks loose as a terrible avalanche: the water, mixed with stones, with blocks of ice, and all the débris torn from its shores, rushes furiously down into the lower valley; it carries away bridges, destroys mills, razes the houses on its banks, washes away the trees on the lower slopes, and lays bare the very meadows as would a huge ploughshare, rolling them all on before it, and mixing them up in the chaos of its deluge. For those valleys through which the inundation sweeps the disaster is enormous, and its story is handed down from generation to generation.

But these are very rare events, and even, in civilized countries, becoming impossible in future; for the menaced population takes care to anticipate the danger by digging subterranean outlets for the lacustrine reservoirs formed behind a shifting dam of ice or stones. Thus kept within bounds, the glacier continues to be the benefactor of the regions situated in the course of its waters. It is the glacier that irrigates them during those seasons when they would have more cause to dread the effects of drought—the glacier that renews them by its contributions of vegetable mould, still quite fresh, and full of its nutritive chemical elements. The glacier is in reality a lake, a sea of fresh water, containing hundreds of thousands of cubic yards; but this lake, suspended on the side of the mountain, makes its escape slowly, and as if by rule. It shuts up water enough to inundate all the lower countries, but it is discreet in dealing out its treasures. Thus this frozen mass, with its death-like aspect, rather adds to the life and fertility of the earth.

Chapter XIV.

FORESTS AND PASTURES.

By its snow and melting ice, which serve to swell the torrents and rivers during the summer, the mountain sustains vegetation at enormous distances from its base, but it keeps back plenty of moisture to nourish its own growth of forests, grass, and moss, so very superior in the number of its species to that of a similar extent of plains. From below our eyes cannot distinguish the details of the picture offered by the verdure of the mountain, but it embraces the magnificent *ensemble,* and enjoys the thousand contrasts which the elevation, the accidents of the ground, the incline of the slopes, the abundance of water, the vicinity of the snow, and all the other physical conditions produce in vegetation.

In spring, when all nature is regenerated, it is delightful to see the green of the grass and foliage prevail over the whiteness of the snow. The blades of grass, which can breathe again, and once more see light, lose their red tint and charred appearance ; they first assume a whitish yellow, then a beautiful green. Multitudes of flowers stud the meadows ; here nothing but ranunculus, elsewhere anemones or primroses, spring up in clusters ; farther away the verdure disappears beneath the snowy white of the graceful narcissus of the poets or the lilac

of the crocus, which is nothing but flower from root to
the tip of the corolla; by the water's side the parnassia
opens its delicate calyx; here and there tiny blue and
white, pink or yellow flowerets are crowded together in
such great numbers that they impart their hues to the
whole of the grassy slope, so that as fast as the snow re-
tires towards the heights before the blooming, verdant
carpet, we can recognize from the opposite declivities
which species of plant predominates in the meadow.
Soon the trees, also, take part in the fête. Below, on
the first slopes, there are fruit-trees, which in a few
weeks' time, after having freed themselves from the
winter's snow, are covered with that of another kind, the
snow of their blossoms. Higher up the chestnuts, the
beeches, the various shrubs, are clad with their tender
green leaves; from day to day the mountain seems to
be freshly clothed with a wondrous tissue, in which silk
and velvet blend. Little by little this youthful verdure
of forests and heaths advances to the summit; it ascends
by the valleys and ravines, as if to scale and conquer the
supreme heights amid the ice. Up there everything assumes an unexpected aspect of gladness. Even the dark
rocks, looking black by contrast with the snow, adorn
the irregularities of their surface with tiny tufts of green.
They, too, take part in the spring-time gayety.

Although less sumptuous in the exuberance of their
verdure and the prodigious multitude of their flowers,
the elevated pastures are more lovely than the meadows
below; their sward is softer, more familiar in its gayety.
We can walk without any exertion on the short turf, and
it is easier to become acquainted with the flowers springing up in myriads among the tufts of verdure. There.

too, the brilliancy of the corollas is incomparable; there the sun darts its most scorching rays with more powerful and more rapid chemical action; in the sap it elaborates coloring substances of the most perfect beauty. Armed with their microscopes, the botanist and physician duly satisfy themselves as to the phenomenon; but, without these instruments, the simple pedestrian can easily perceive with his naked eye that the blue of no flower in the plain equals the deep cerulean hue of the little gentian. Eager to live and to enjoy, the plants make themselves as beautiful as possible. They don the most vivid hues, for the season of gladness will be short. When the summer has swiftly fled, death will overtake them.

Our sight is dazzled with the radiancy presented by wide patches of turf studded with the vivid pink stars of the catch-fly, the blue clusters of the myosotis, the big golden-hearted flowers of the alpine asters. Upon the driest slopes, among arid rocks, grows the black orchis, with its perfume of vanilla, and the "lion's-foot," whose flower never fades, and for lovers remains a symbol of eternal love.

Among these plants, with their brilliant bloom, there are some which are not in the least afraid either of the snow or the frozen water. They are not at all chilly; close beside the crystals of the snow-bank the flow of the sap circulates freely through the tissues of the delicate soldanella, as it bends its tender, pure-hued corolla over the snow. When the sun shines, we may say of it, with more reason than of the palm-tree in the oasis, that its foot is in ice and its head in fire. Even at the outlet of the snow, the torrent, whose milky water seems to be

composed of barely melted ice, folds in its arms a blooming islet, a charming bouquet, with ever-shivering stems.
Farther on the bed of snow, shielded from the sun's rays
by the shadow of the rock, is dotted all over with flowers; the soft temperature which they shed has thawed
the surrounding ice; they seem to spring from a crystal
chalice whose base the shadow has dyed blue. Other
more sensitive flowers dare not undergo immediate contact with the snow, but take care to surround themselves
with a soft robe of moss; they are like rubies reposing
upon a green-velvet cushion in the centre of a white
downy bed.

Forests alternate with the grassy surface on the mountain's sides, but not at haphazard. The presence of big
trees always indicates sufficiently deep vegetable mould
and abundance of water for irrigation upon the slopes
which produce them; thus, thanks to the distribution of
forests and pastures, we can read from afar some of the
mountain's secrets, provided, at least, that man has not
rudely interfered by hewing down the trees and modifying the aspect of the heights. There are whole regions
where man, greedy to enrich himself, has cut down every
tree; not even a stump remains, for the winter's snow,
no longer arrested by the living barrier, can henceforth
slide freely down during the season of the avalanches;
it denudes the ground, planes it away to the rock, dragging with it all the remains of the roots.

The ancient feeling of veneration has almost disappeared. Formerly the woodcutter never approached a
forest without dread; the wind which he heard sighing
was for him as the voice of the gods; supernatural beings were concealed beneath the oak, and the sap of the

tree was equally divine blood. When obliged to lay the axe to the trunks, he did it in trembling: "**If** thou art a god, if thou art a goddess," would **say the** Apennine mountaineer—"if thou art a **god, pardon me;**" and he would repeat the prayers **ordained; but was he** reassured after these genuflections?

While swinging his axe, **he saw the** branches wave to and fro above his head; the wrinkles of the bark appeared to assume an **angry expression, to be** animated by a terrible glance; at the first blow the moist **wood** might have been the rosy flesh **of a nymph.** "**No doubt** the priest has sanctioned, **but what will the divinity say?** Will not the **axe suddenly rebound, and** plunge into the body of him **who wields it?**"

Some trees are still worshipped; the mountaineer does not know why, and does not like to be interrogated on that point; but still, in many places, we see oaks respected by the inhabitants, who have surrounded them with palings, to protect them against animals and wandering travellers. In ancient Brittany, when a man was in danger of death, and no priest was to be found in the vicinity, he might make his confession **at the foot of a** tree; **the branches** heard, and their rustling bore **the dy**ing man's last prayer to heaven.

All the same, if here and there some venerable trunk is respected, in memory of olden times, the forest itself no longer inspires holy terror; in our days the woodcutters do not stand upon such ceremony as their ancestors, especially when not making an onslaught on woods serving as a barrier against avalanches. It is sufficient for them if only they can cultivate the trees in a profitable manner; that is to say, gain more by the sale of the

timber than they have to expend on cutting down and
transporting it. Numbers of forests still stand in their
primeval virgin state, owing to the difficulty the culti-
vator finds in reaching them and sending away the cut-
down trees. But when the means of access are easy,
when the mountains offer good slides down which, with
one single push, hundreds of yards of dismantled trunks
can be sent; when, at the foot of the slope, the torrent
in the valley is strong enough to carry the trees in rafts
as far as the plains, or to be able to turn powerful mechanical saws, then the forests run great risk of being
attacked by wood-cutters. If they cultivate intelligently,
if they carefully regulate their cutting in such a manner
as always to leave harvests of wood standing for the following years, and to develop in the forest ground the
greatest possible power of production, man has but to
congratulate himself upon the new riches he obtains.
But when he hews down and destroys the whole forest
at one blow, as if seized with a fit of frenzy, is not one
tempted to curse?

The beauty of the forests still left to us upon the
mountain slopes makes us regret all the more those of
which violent speculators have robbed us. Upon the
first slopes, near the plains, clumps of chestnuts have
been spared, thanks to their leaves, which the peasants
collect for their cattle's litter, and to their fruit, which
the people themselves eat of a winter's evening. Few
forests, even in the tropical regions, where we see trees
of the most diverse natures alternate, present greater
picturesqueness and variety than do chestnut-woods. The
turf-clad slopes extended at the foot of the trees are sufficiently clear from brushwood to permit many views be-

neath the spreading branches to be freely opened out before our gaze. In many places the verdant vault allows
the light of heaven to pass through; the gray of the
shadows and **the** soft yellow of the rays flicker with the
motion of the foliage; the mosses and lichens covering
the rough bark with their mantle add to the sweetness of
these fugitive lights and shadows. The trees themselves
either rise up solitarily or in groups of two or three, differing in form and aspect. Almost **all,** by the grooves
in their bark and the spreading of their boughs, seem to
have been subjected to **a sort of** twisting from left to
right; but while some possess tolerably smooth boles and
regularly bifurcated branches, others display curious protuberances, knots, excrescences, strangely adorned with
tufts of leaves. There are old trees, with enormous trunks,
which have lost all their big branches beneath the violence of storms, and have replaced them by little twigs
pointed like spears; others have retained their boughs,
but have decayed internally; **time has** gnawed away
their stems by hollowing **out** deep cavities; sometimes
nothing **is left but a** simple shell of wood, covered with
bark, to bear the whole weight of the upper growth.
Here and there, **too,** upon the ground we notice the remains of a bolé of mighty dimensions; the tree itself has
disappeared, but all around this vegetable ruin chestnut-
trees grow singly, which were formerly united in the gigantic colonnade, and are now isolated, shrunken, limit-
ed to their meagre individuality. Thus the forest offers
the greatest variety; side by side with well-grown trees,
superb in aspect and majestic in carriage, are groups
whose singular forms evoke before our imagination the
monsters of fables or dreams.

Far less varied in their manners are the beeches, which delight in forming a forest as much as do the chestnuts. Almost all are upright as columns, and long open spaces between their shafts allow our gaze to extend far away. The beeches are smooth with radiant bark and lichens ; only at the bottom are they clad with green moss; little tufts of leaves here and there adorn the lower part of the stem ; but it is about fifteen yards above the ground that the branches begin to spread out and unite tree to tree in one continued vault, pierced by parallel rays fleck- ing the ground. The forest's aspect is severe, yet hospi- table ; a soft light composed of all these radiant clusters, dyed green by the reflections of the leaves, fills the ave- nue and blends with their gloom, producing a vague ash- en-hued day, void of all flashes of light and yet of all darkness. In this light we can clearly distinguish every- thing living at the foot of these great trees: the creep- ing insects, the tiny waving flowers, the fungi and moss- es carpeting the soil and roots ; but upon the trees them- selves the white or golden-yellow lichens and rays are mingled in confusion. The beech forest constantly changes its aspect, according to the season. When au- tumn comes, its foliage is tinted with a diversity of hues wherein brown and red shades predominate ; it then with- ers and falls to the ground, covering this with thick beds of dried leaves, quivering in the least breath of air. The sunlight penetrates freely into the forest between its bare branches, but so do the snow and fog ; the wood remains sad and melancholy until spring arrives, when its early flowers open out beside the flakes of melting snow, when the blushing buds spread over the branches like a vague gleam of dawn.

The forest of firs, growing at the same elevation as the beeches upon the mountain's side, but in a different situation, is gloomy and forbidding in a very dissimilar manner. It seems to be guarding some terrible secret; dull noises issue from its branches, then die away, to be renewed again like the distant murmuring of waves. But it is up above, among the boughs, that this noise is propagated; below all is calm, impassive, sinister; the branches, laden with their dark foliage, bend almost to the ground; we shudder as we pass beneath these gloomy vaults. When winter loads their stalwart boughs with snow, they will not give way, or allow more than a silvery dust to fall upon the sward. Any one would say that these trees possessed a tenacious will, the more powerful in that they are all dominated by one and the same idea. When climbing up through the forest to the summit of the mountain, we see that the trees have to make a greater struggle to keep themselves alive in the chilly atmosphere. Their bark is rougher, their trunks less straight, their branches more gnarled, their foliage harder, less abundant; they could not resist the snow, the tempests, the cold, save for the shelter which they furnish one another; isolated, they would perish; united as a forest, they continue to live. Yet when, on the side of the peak, the trees forming the first defensive palisade begin to give way at any one point, their neighbors are soon shaken and thrown down by the storm. The forest presents itself as an army, placing its trees in a row like soldiers in battle array. Only one or two firs, more robust than the rest, remain in front like champions. Securely anchored upon the rock, resting upon their thickset loins, covered with wrinkles and knots as if with ar-

mor, they defy the storm, and here and there proudly
shake their little plume of leaves. I saw one of these
heroes who had taken possession of an isolated peak, and
thence overlooked an immense tract of dales and ravines.
Its roots, which the very shallow vegetable mould had
not been able to cover, enveloped the rock for a great
distance; creeping and tortuous as serpents, they unite
again in a single low gnarled trunk, which seemed to take
possession of the mountain. The branches of the struggling tree had become contorted beneath the efforts of
the wind; but, firmly united, they can still brave the onslaught of a hundred tempests.

Trees will still grow above the forest of pines and its
little outpost, exposed to every storm; but they are of a
species which, far from soaring straight up to heaven,
rather creep along the ground, and glide timidly into the
surface irregularities to escape from the wind and cold.
They develop in breadth; the branches, serpentine as
the roots, stretch out above them and take advantage of
the small amount of heat radiating from them; it is thus
that sheep crowd up one against another to keep warm
during the winter nights. By making themselves small,
and presenting but slight resistance to the storm and a
small surface to the cold, the juniper-trees of the mountain succeed in preserving their existence: we still see
them creeping towards the snowy summits, hundreds of
yards above the fir, daring as it is in its ascent. In the
same way, shrubs, such as alpine roses and heaths, con-
trive to raise themselves to great altitudes; owing to the
spherical or domelike form possessed by all the stems
pressed close up together, the wind readily passes over
these vegetable balls. Higher up, however, indeed, they

are obliged to relinquish their conflict with the cold; they **give** place to the mosses **spreading** out over the **ground, to** the lichens incorporating themselves with the rock. From the stone vegetation came, to it vegetation must return.

CHAPTER XV.

THE ANIMALS OF THE MOUNTAIN.

RICH in its growth of forests, shrubs, grass, and moss, the mountain seems to be very poor in animals; it would appear to be almost utterly deserted had shepherds not led to it their herds of cattle and flocks of sheep, which we can see a great way off upon the green pastures like red or white specks, and if the ever-zealous sheep-dogs did not incessantly run from right to left, making the rocks resound with their barking. They are temporary emigrants who have come up from the low plains in spring-time, and must return there in the winter, unless they be concealed in the depths of cattle-sheds in the hamlets of the valley. The only children of the mountain to be met with while climbing the acclivities are insects crossing the footpaths and gliding through the grass; butterflies, among which we see the black Erebus, with its changing reflections, and the magnificent Apollo, that living flower fluttering above other flowers, are buzzing in the air; here and there some reptile steals away between two stones. The forests are very mute; rarely are birds to be heard singing in them.

Yet the mountain, a natural fortress rising up in the midst of plains, has its visitors too; some, timid fugitives seeking an inaccessible retreat; others, daring robbers,

beasts of prey, which, from the height of their watch-
towers, scan the horizon from afar before rushing out
upon their pillaging expeditions. It is a strange fact,
teaching us only too well to understand man's cowardice,
that the beasts of the mountain which destroy and kill
one another are precisely those which we most admire.
We should readily convert them into kings; and in all
myths, fables, legends, and many an old book of natural
history, that name is really given to them.

To begin with, there are the eagle and other rapacious
birds of prey, which all the lords of the earth have
chosen as emblems, sometimes endowing them with two
heads, as if they themselves would like to have two beaks
wherewith to devour. The eagle is beautiful when he is
proudly perched upon a rock, inaccessible to man, and
much more magnificent still when he sails tranquilly
through the air, lord of the skies; but what signifies his
beauty? If the king admires, the shepherd hates him.
He is the enemy of the flock, and its keeper has vowed
war to the death against him. Soon, eagles, vultures,
and griffins shall exist nowhere, save in our museums;
even now in many mountains not a single nest is to be
seen, or, if one does remain, it contains but a solitary de-
fiant bird, so old as to be semi-impotent, and to be eaten
up by parasites.

The bear is also a destroyer of sheep; and, sooner or
later, the shepherd will exterminate him in our mountains. Despite his prodigious strength, and the skill with
which he can crush bones, he is not the favorite of kings,
who doubtlessly do not consider him sufficiently graceful
to assign to him a place in their escutcheons; but, on the
other hand, many a tribe cherishes him for the sake of

his qualities. And even the huntsman who pursues cannot resist a certain affection for him. The Ostiak, after having dealt his death-blow and having stretched him bleeding on the snow, throws himself upon his knees before the corpse to implore its forgiveness: " I have killed you, O my God! but I was hungry, my family was hungry, and you are so good that you will pardon my crime." Yet the bear does not impress us as being a deity; but how honest, frank, and benevolent he seems! How he appears to practise all the family virtues! How gentle he is towards his young, and how gay, frisky, and frolicsome are they! We must go to the bear's den, or his enormous lair comfortably carpeted with moss, to find those patriarchal customs which have been so greatly vaunted. It is true that from time to time the huge animal gives a fatal bite to the shepherd's flock; but is he not, as a rule, sobriety itself? He contents himself with browsing on leaves, feeding on whortleberries, devouring combs of honey; perhaps he may even venture down into the valley, calmly to eat grapes and pears. A Swiss naturalist, Tsendi, asserts, upon his honor, that if, on his way, the honest beast should meet a little girl carrying a basket of strawberries, he would content himself with delicately placing his paw upon the basket to ask for his share. And when he has entered man's employment he is willing, good-humored, magnanimous, and contemptuous of insults! I cannot refrain from regretting this good beast, whom we shall soon see no more in our mountains, and whose paws the huntsman proudly nails up against his barn-door. The race will be suppressed, but with what superior intelligence might we not have tamed and admitted him to take part in our labors?

As to the wolf, no one will regret him when he shall have entirely disappeared from the mountain. He is a thoroughly malevolent, perfidious, sanguinary, cowardly, vile fellow. He thinks of nothing but tearing his victim to pieces, and drinking the warm blood as it flows from the wound. All animals hate him, and he hates them; yet he only ventures to attack the feeble and wounded. The madness of hunger alone urges him to throw himself upon those who are stronger than himself. But then with what eagerness does he rush upon a fallen prey, an enemy who cannot defend himself! Even when a wolf falls, still alive, beneath the huntsman's bullet, all his companions cast themselves upon him to complete the work and to quarrel over his carcass. Certainly blood-thirsty Rome has charged her memory with all imaginable crimes; she has razed thousands of towns, destroyed millions of human beings, gorged herself with the earth's riches. By violence and perfidy, by infamies without number, she became the queen of the ancient world; and yet, in spite of all her crimes, she has calumniated herself by claiming a she-wolf as her mother and patroness. That people, whose laws under another guise still govern us, were certainly hard, almost ferocious, but yet not so bad as the symbol chosen by them would lead us to believe.

It is a satisfaction for any one who loves the mountain to know that the wolf, that odious creature, is an animal belonging to wide plains. The destruction of his native forests and the increasing number of huntsmen have obliged him to seek refuge in the gorges of the heights, but he is none the less an intruder; he is so organized as to be able to perform, in one stage, journeys of fifty miles across the steppes, not to climb the acclivities of rocks. The animal, the form of whose body and the elasticity of whose muscles render him best adapted for springing from rock to rock, for crossing crevasses, is the graceful chamois, the antelope of our countries. He is the true inhabitant of the mountain; no precipice alarms, no slope of snow stays him; in a few bounds he climbs dizzy escarpments where the most eager huntsman dare not venture. With one leap he springs on to points smaller than the space which his four feet, closely put together, would cover; certainly he is an animal belonging to the earth, but any one would believe him to be winged. Then, too, he is gentle and sociable; he would love to mingle with our flocks of goats and sheep. No doubt, a few efforts would suffice to add him to our small category of domestic animals; but it is easier to kill than to rear him, and the few chamois still left are reserved for the delight of sportsmen. In all probability, that race will soon disappear. After all, is it not better to die than to live a slave?

Other animals have chosen their dwelling higher still than the chamois, upon the slopes and rocks surrounded on every side by snow. One of them is a species of hare, which has understood cunningly to change his livery in such a manner, according to the season, as always to be indistinguishable from the surrounding soil. It is thus that he escapes the eagle's piercing eye. In winter, when all the slopes are clad with snow, his fur is as white as the flakes; in spring, tufts of plants and pebbles appear here and there through the snowy bed, simultaneously the animal's coat becomes dotted with gray spots; in summer he is the color of stones and burnt-up grass;

"THE GRACEFUL CHAMOIS."

then, with the sudden change of season, he again as suddenly changes his skin. Still better protected, the marmot passes his winter in a deep hole, where the temperature always remains equable, in spite of the thick layers
of snow covering the ground; and during whole months
he suspends the course of his life, until the perfume of
flowers and the rays of spring come to awaken him from
his lethargic sleep. At last, one of those ever-active, ever-
wakeful rodents which we encounter everywhere has
undertaken to reach the summit of the mountains by
hollowing out tunnels and galleries beneath the snow—I
mean a field-mouse. Covered with this cold mantle, he
seeks his meagre nourishment in the ground, and, wonderful to relate, finds it!

Such is the fertility of the earth that it brings forth,
for the incessant battle of life, populations of consumers
and victims who carry on their conflicts in obscurity
more than a thousand yards above the limit of perpetual
snow! Here again, beneath the beds of the frozen earth,
I find once more that terrible struggle for existence, the
almost invariably hideous spectacle of which had driven
me from the plains.

Frequently the bird of prey soars higher still, but it is
to travel from one mountain slope to another, or to gaze
far away over the extensive country and to discover his
quarry. The butterflies and dragon-flies, carried away
by the delight of flying up towards the sun, sometimes
ascend as far as the loftiest zone of the mountains, and,
without foreseeing the cold of the night, do not cease
gayly to mount towards the light. More frequently still
those poor little creatures, such as flies and other insects,
are carried off to the lofty peaks by hurricanes, and their

7

remains, mingled with the dust, are strewn over the surface of the snow. But in addition to these strangers
who, either voluntarily or by force, visit the regions of silence and death, there are other indigenous dwellers who
are quite at home there; they do not find the atmosphere too cold or the ground too hardly frozen. The
immense dreary tract of snow lies extended around them;
but the points of the rocks, which here and there pierce
the snowy couch, are for them an oasis in the midst of
the desert : it is there, no doubt, among these lichens, that
they find the nourishment necessary for their subsistence.
It is marvellous how they thrive, and naturalists ascer-
tain the fact with astonishment.

Spiders, insects, or snow-maggots—all these tiny creatures must know hunger; and perhaps the divers phenomena of their life are effected extremely slowly. In this
region of hoar-frost the chrysalides must remain a long
time buried in their apparent sleep of death.

Not only does life exhibit itself by the side of snow,
but the snow itself appears animate in certain places, so
greatly do these animalcula multiply. Far away we see
great red or yellow spots on the white expanse. It is the
snow rotting, the mountaineers say; they arise, say the
savants, armed with microscopes, from millions and millions of crawling creatures, who live, love, propagate, and
eat one another up.

Chapter XVI.

GRADATIONS OF CLIMATE.

Those naturalists who wander about the mountain, studying the living creatures, plants, or animals inhabiting it, do not confine themselves to studying each species in its actual form and habits; they also desire to know the extent of its domain, the general distribution of its representatives upon the slopes, and the history of its race. They consider the countless creatures of each species—plants, insects, or mammalia—as one immense individual, whose abodes on the surface of the earth, and whose duration during the course of ages, we ought thoroughly to understand.

In climbing up the side of a mountain, the traveller first remarks how very few are the plants which accompany him to the summit. Those which he saw at the bottom, and on the lower levels, he does not meet again upon the more elevated slopes; or, if a few should still exist there, they disappear in the vicinity of the snow, to be replaced by other species. It is one constant change in the aspect of the flora as we approach the frigid peaks. But when a plant indigenous to the lower hills continues to exhibit itself beside the footpath close to the snow, it appears gradually to change; down below, the flower has already faded, while on the heights it is hardly yet

in bud; here it has already spent its summer, yonder up
above it is yet in spring.

We could not measure with a cord the exact elevation
at which this plant ceases to grow and that one makes
its first appearance. A thousand conditions of soil and
climate labor incessantly to displace, to widen, or to con-
tract the limits separating the natural domains of the various species. When the ground changes, rock succeeding soil, or clay replacing sand, a great number of plants
also give way to one another. Contrasts bring about
similar results; as, for instance, whether water washes
away the earth, or there is a deficiency of it in the
parched-up ground; whether the wind whistles freely in
all its fury, or it encounters obstacles acting as protec-
tion against its violence. At the outlet of those necks
of mountains where the hurricanes blow hardest, certain
slopes are so completely swept by the bitter blast that
trees and shrubs as suddenly cease to grow beneath this
formidable breeze as they would before a wall of ice.
Elsewhere the vegetation varies according to the steepness of the slopes. Nothing but moss grows upon vertical cliffs; brushwood only can find a footing upon the
dry, steep walls of precipices; where the incline, although less sharp, is yet inaccessible to man, trees creep
along rocks and anchor their roots in the fissures; on
the other hand, upon the terraces their trunks rise up
erectly, and their foliage spreads out. The nature of the
trees usually varies as greatly as their elevation. Wherever the difference of the slopes is caused by the rocky
strata, being more or less injured by atmospheric agents,
the mountain presents a succession of parallel tiers of
vegetation of the most curious effect. Both stones and
plants change in regular alternations.

"FIR-TREES, WITH THEIR SOMBRE BRANCHES."

Of all the contrasts of vegetation, the most important, upon the whole, is that which is caused by the different degrees of exposure to the sun's rays. How many times —when penetrating into a very regular valley, overlooked by uniform slopes, the one turned to the north, the other exposed to the due south—can we see how this difference of light and heat modifies vegetation on the two sides of the mountain! The contrast is frequently absolute; they might be two regions of the earth some hundreds of miles apart. On one side are fruit-trees, cultivated lands, rich meadows; facing it, nor fields nor gardens, nothing but woods and pastures. Even the forests growing on the two opposite slopes consist of totally different species. Up yonder, beneath the pale light reflected by the northern skies, are fir-trees with their sombre branches; beneath the life-giving brilliancy of the south are larches of a tender green, luxuriant as an immense espalier. Man, as have these plants which strive to expand beneath the sun's rays, has chosen for his abode the slopes turned towards the south. On yonder side houses border the roads in one almost continued line; snug cottages are scattered, like gray rocks, upon the upper pastures. On the other cold side rising up facing it, hardly a single little house is to be seen sheltering itself within the bend of a ravine.

Very different are the mountain slopes in aspect, climate, and vegetation; yet all possess this phenomenon in common, that in ascending them we might imagine we were going towards the poles of the world: if we climb up a hundred yards, we seem as if we were transported fifty miles farther away from the equator. Yonder peak which we see rising above our heads contains a flora sim-

ilar to that of Scandinavia. Let us pass that point to rise
still higher, and we enter Lapland; at another still greater altitude we find the vegetation of Spitzbergen. Each
mountain is, in its plants, a sort of recapitulation of all
the country extending from its base to the polar regions,
across continents and oceans. Botanists, in their narra-
tions, often evince the joy, the emotion, they feel when,
after having climbed the naked rocks, crossed the snow,
walked beside yawning chasms, they at last reach a free
spot, a "garden," whose blooming plants remind them
of some beloved distant northern land, their own country
perhaps, situated millions of yards away. The miracle
of the "Thousand and One Nights" is being realized for
them at the cost of some hours' walking; here they are
transported into another nature, beneath another climate.

Every year some violent but temporary disturbances
are produced in this regular stratification of flowers.
When walking amid the most recent landslips, or upon
the accumulations of earth brought by the torrents from
the top of the mountains, the botanist frequently ob-
serves some confusion in the distribution of the vegetable tribes; these are phenomena which affect him, for
the result of studying plants is that he ends by sympa-
thizing with them. This sight, making his heart beat,
is caused by the forcible expatriation of plants and
mosses violently carried away into a climate for which
they were not created. In their fall or descent from the
top of the upper slopes, the rocks brought with them
their flowers, seeds, roots, whole stems. As would the
fragments of a distant planet which might land the inhabitants of another world upon the earth, these rocks,
descended from the summit, serve as a means of convey-

ance for colonies of plants. The poor little things, astonished to be breathing another atmosphere, to find themselves amid other conditions of cold and heat, of dryness and moisture, of light and shadow, strive to become acclimatized in their new country. Some strangers succeed in holding their own against the throng of native plants surrounding them, but the greatest number have hard work to form themselves into groups, to keep close together like refugees; hated by all the world, and loving one another all the more fondly, they are doomed soon to perish. Attacked on every side by the ancient possessors of the soil, they end by relinquishing the place which the fall of their mother-rock had obliged them to take by force. The botanist, studying them in their novel surroundings, sees them perish by degrees; after some years' sojourn, the colonies are composed of but a small number of miserable individuals, then even these remaining creatures are finally extinguished. It is thus that in our human race strange colonies successively die in the midst of a people which hates them, and beneath a climate that is adverse to them.

Despite temporary irregularities, the stratification of flowers upon the mountains' sides does, after all, preserve the character of a steadfast law.

Whence proceeds this strange distribution of plants on the globe's surface? Why have the original species of the most distant countries thus herded in tiny colonies on the high slopes of mountains? No doubt the pollen of some may have been carried by birds, or even by stormy winds; but most of these species possess seeds on which no birds feed, and which are too heavy to have adhered to their feathers or claws. Among those plants

from the cold regions which colonize the mountain there
are even **entire families growing from** bulbs ; and cer-
tainly neither wind nor birds could have carried them
across continents and seas.

Thus, then, these **plants** must have been propagated
from one place to another **by gradual** encroachment, as
they are in our fields and meadows. Small colonists
whom **we now see in the high "gardens"** surrounded
with snow have slowly ascended **from the lower plains ;**
while other plants of the same species, moving in a contrary direction, bend their steps towards the polar regions
where they are now located.   No doubt, then, the cli-
mate of our fields was as cold as **is in our** days that of
the most elevated summits and of the boreal zone ; but
little by little the temperature becomes softer, the plants
which luxuriated in **the rude, cold breeze** were obliged
to take flight, **the one to** the **north, the** other to the
slopes of the mountains.   **Of these** two fugitive bands,
separated **by an** unceasingly **increasing zone, occupied by**
hostile species, the one, that which retreated towards the
mountains, beheld **the space diminishing before it pro-**
portionately with the augmenting mildness of **the cli-**
mate : first it occupied the lower chains of the base, then
the medium points, then the lofty peaks, and now some
have for their last refuge the supreme ridges of the
mountain.   **When** the climate **becomes** cold again, in
consequence of some cosmical change, the little plants
will recommence their journeys towards the plain ; victorious in their turn, they will drive away before them
the species demanding a milder temperature.   According to the alternations of their climates and of their immense cycles, the armies of plants advance or retire along

the surface of the globe, leaving behind them bands of laggards which reveal to us what was formerly the route of the main body.

The same phenomena exist among human tribes as in those of plants and animals. During the variations of the climate, the people of the different races who could not accommodate themselves to the changing medium moved slowly northward or southward, driven away by the cold or excessive heat. Unhappily, history, which had not then begun to exist, has not been able to relate to us this wandering to and fro of the different peoples; besides which, in his great migrations, man invariably obeys a variety of passions which he cannot analyze. How many tribes have thus moved and changed their dwelling without knowing what was urging them forward! They then related, in their traditions, how they had been guided by a star or a pillar of fire—even how they had followed the flight of an eagle, or planted their feet in the tracks left by the *sabot* of a bison.

If history is mute, or at least very reticent, as to the marches and counter-marches imposed upon the people by the changes of climate, it suffices, on the other hand, to see how, upon the opposite sides of most of the mountains, the differences among men respond to those of the temperature and of the atmosphere. When the contrast of climate on each side of the mountain is very slight, either because the direction of the whole range of heights is from north to south, or because winds of the same origin, and bringing the same amount of moisture, irrigate the same slopes, then the men of one and the same race can spread freely from one part to another; give themselves up to the same culture, the same industries, practise the same customs. The wall rising up between them, and which is, perhaps, interrupted with numerous breaches, is not a separating rampart. But when, every here and there, one of the slopes belonging to the mountain, and the whole series of summits attached to it, are turned to the north and its cold winds, while the opposite incline receives an abundance of soft rays from the south; or, again, when on one side the vapors of the sea pour down in torrents, while on the other side the ravines always remain dry, then, certainly, flora, fauna, and humanity, on both sides, will present the most remarkable contrasts. Each step made by the traveller after he has attained the crest places him in the presence of a new nature; he penetrates into another world, where discovery succeeds discovery. Now he stops before a sweet-smelling plant which he had never seen; a strange butterfly flutters before him; while he is studying new species, vegetable or animal, or is seeking to explain to himself all the features of this hitherto unknown nature, a shepherd comes towards him: it is a man of different race, of different civilization—his very speech is different.

While separating two zones of climate, the crest of the mountain thus also separates two nations: it is a constant phenomenon in all countries of the world where conquest has not ruthlessly mixed or suppressed the races; and, even in spite of the violence of conquests, this normal contrast between the populations of the two sides has been frequently re-established. Take, for instance, the history of Italy. The splendor of this country fascinated the barbarians of the north and northeast. How often have the German and French people, attracted by the riches of its territory, by the treasures of its towns, the flavor of its fruits, the beauty of its women, flung themselves in armed bands upon the plains surrounded by the stupendous barrier of the Alps! In vain have they massacred, burned, destroyed; in vain installed themselves in the places of the vanquished; built towns and constructed citadels for themselves; the native population has always resumed its power, and the strangers, Celts or Teutons, have been obliged to recross the Alps.

The mountains, too, relatively insignificant protuberances on the surface of the globe, simple obstacles which man can ordinarily cross in one day, acquire great historical importance as the natural frontiers between the different nations. They owe this rôle in the life of mankind less to the want of roads, to the steepness of their escarpments, to their zone of snow and sterile rocks, than to the diversity, and frequently to the hostility, of the populations seated at the two opposite bases. The history of the past teaches us that every natural boundary placed between two peoples, in the form of an obstacle difficult to surmount—be it plateau, mountain, desert, or river—was at the same time a moral frontier for mankind; just as, in fairy tales, people fortified themselves with an invisible wall, erected by hatred and contempt. Any man coming from beyond the mountains was not merely a stranger, he was an enemy. The nations hated one another; but sometimes a shepherd, superior to all his race, would sweetly sing some simple words of love while gazing far away beyond the mountains. He, at least, knew how to surmount the lofty barrier of rocks and snow; by means of his heart he knew how to make a home for himself on both sides of the mountain. One of our old Pyrenean songs relates this triumph of love over nature, and over the traditions of national hatred :

"Baicha-bous, montagnes! Planos, haoussa-bous;
Daqué pousqui bede oun soun mas amous!"

"Baissez-vous, montagnes! plaines, haussez-vous;
Et que je puisse voir où sont mes amours!"

Chapter XVII.

THE FREE MOUNTAINEER.

The crumpling-up of the terrestrial surface into mountains and valleys is thus a leading feature in the history of nations, and often it explains their journeys, their migrations, their conflicts, their various destinies; it is thus that a molehill, rising up in a meadow, in the midst of eager populations of insects hurrying to and fro, immediately changes all their plans, and causes the route of the travelling tribes to diverge in various directions.

While its enormous mass separates the nations besetting the slopes on every side, the mountain also protects the inhabitants, usually very few in number, who have come to seek refuge in its valleys. It shelters them, it makes them its own, imposes special customs upon them, a certain style of life, a peculiar character. Whatsoever may have been his original race, the mountaineer has become such as he is beneath the influence of his surroundings; the fatigue of the ascents and toilsome descents, the simplicity of his food, the rigor of the winter's cold, the struggles with hardships, have made an exceptional man of him—have imparted to him carriage, gait, and movements very different from those of his neighbors in the plains. Besides this, they have endowed him with a mode of thinking and feeling which distinguishes him;

they have reflected in his mind, as in that of the sailor, something of the serenity of great horizons; in many places, also, they have guaranteed him the inappreciable treasure of liberty.

One of the great causes contributing to maintain the independence of certain mountain tribes is that, for them, mutual assistance in work and combined efforts are a necessity. All are useful to each, and each is useful to all; the shepherd, who goes to the elevated pastures to watch flocks belonging to the community, is not least necessary to the general prosperity. When any disaster takes place, all are obliged to give their help to repair the evil: an avalanche has buried some cabins, all work at removing the snow; the rain has made ravines in the fields cultivated in terraces on the slopes, all busy themselves to restore the earth that has slipped down into the bottoms, and bring it back in basketfuls to the declivities whence it fell down; the overflowing torrent has covered the meadows with pebbles, all are employed in freeing the grass from the débris which smothers it. In winter, when it is dangerous to venture into the snow, they count upon each other's hospitality; they are all brothers; they are members of one family. Just the same when they are attacked; they resist with one accord; are stirred, so to say, by one single idea. Moreover, the life of incessant struggles, of unbroken combats with dangers of every kind—perhaps, too, the pure, healthy air which they breathe — makes hardy, death-despising men of them. Peaceable toilers, they never attack, yet they know how to defend themselves.

The protecting mountain provides them with the means to shield themselves against invasion. It defends the valley by narrow defiles, where a few men would suffice to guard the entrance against whole bands; it conceals its fertile vales in the hollows of lofty terraces, whose escarpments appear to be insurmountable; in certain places it is perforated with caverns communicating with each other, and capable of serving as hiding-places.

Upon the wall of a defile which I frequently visited stood one of these hidden fortresses. It was with the greatest difficulty that I could reach the entrance, by clinging to the fissures of the rock, and by calling to my aid several stems of boxwood, which had inserted their roots in the clefts. How much more difficult would the escalade have been for besiegers! Blocks of rock piled up before the entrance to the cave were ready to roll and rebound from point to point down to the very torrent. On each side of the entrance the rock, absolutely upright and polished, did not leave room for an adder to slip through; above, the cliff overhung, and like a gigantic porch protected the aperture. In addition to this, a great wall half shut it in. Thus, then, unless taken by surprise, the grotto was unapproachable for all assailants. The enemy would be obliged to limit themselves to keeping watch from afar; but when at last, hearing not the slightest sound come forth, they finally ventured in to count the bodies, they would find the subterranean galleries perfectly empty. The occupants had glided from cavern to cavern, until they reached another still more secret place of egress amid the brushwood. The chase had to commence afresh. Sometimes, alas! it terminated in the capture of the game. Man is the prey of man.

In certain localities, where the mountain does not offer propitious cavities, an isolated rock in the valley, one

with upright facets, would serve as a fortress. Cut per-
pendicularly on the three sides whose base is surrounded
by the torrent, it was inaccessible excepting from one
quarter; and on that side the little troop of mountaineers
who desired to make it both their watch-tower and their
hiding-place, in case of retreat, had but to continue the
work begun by nature. They cut away the rock, rendered it impassable for human footsteps, and left but one single subterranean entrance hewn out of the thickness of
the rock with a crow-bar. Once they had entered their
eyry, the inhabitants of the fortress blocked up the entrance by means of huge pieces of rock; a bird only was
thus able to pay them a visit. Architecture was not at
all needed for this citadel. Perhaps, however, from a
species of coquetry, the mountaineer would border the
edge of the precipice with a crenellated wall, which permitted his children safely to play upon the whole extent
of the plateau, and from whose top he could more easily
spy out everything showing itself on any portion of the
mountain's slopes. In many mountainous countries of
the East, where the valleys are peopled with races hostile
to one another, and where, consequently, the murder of
a man is esteemed a mere peccadillo, numbers of these
rocky fortresses are still inhabited. When a guest arrives at the foot of the escarpment, he announces his
presence by shouting. Thereupon a basket descends
through an open trap in the rock, the traveller gets into
it, and the stalwart arms of his friends above slowly hoist
up the heavy conveyance as it gyrates in the air.

If the abrupt rocks of the high valleys served to defend peaceable populations against all incursions, the
little protuberances of the plain, on the other hand,

acted as watch and pillage stations for some predatory baron.

How many villages, even in our country, show by their architecture that until quite recently war was permanent, and that at every moment it was necessary to expect an attack from lords or brigands! There are no isolated houses on the hill-sides void of means of defence; all the hovels, like sheep frightened by the storm, have been huddled together, resembling one vast heap of stones. From below it looks like a mere continuation of the rock, an indentation of the summit, now shining in the light, now black in the shadow; it is approached by dizzy steps, which each morning the peasants must descend to cultivate their fields, which they must wearily ascend each evening after the day's long toil. One entrance alone gives access to the hamlet, and upon the side towers can still be seen the traces of portcullises and other means of defence; not one window looks out over the expanse of the surrounding valleys; the only openings are loop-holes, through which formerly passed javelins and the muzzles of guns. Even nowadays the descendants of these unhappy people, besieged generation after generation, are afraid to build their dwellings in the middle of their fields. They could have done so, but custom, of all tyrants that which receives most obedience, still pens them up in the ancient prison.

The higher valleys of the mountain were free to the mountaineers; but outside the narrow passages, wherein no aggressor had ever ventured with impunity, an almost isolated cliff bore the strong castle of a baron. From up yonder, the brigand, ennobled by his own crimes and by those of his ancestors, could command the surrounding

plains as well as the ravines and defiles of the mountain.
Like a serpent coiled up on a rock, and raising its restless
head to watch a nestful of tiny birds, the bandit watches
from the height of his keep; he dare not attack the
mountaineers in their valley, but at least he promises
himself to surprise and subdue those who venture into
the plain.

The castle belonging to the noble destroyer of all way-
farers now lies in ruins. A stony footpath obstructed
by briers has replaced the road along which the warriors
made their glad horses caracole when setting out upon
an expedition, up which toiled the captive merchants in
chains, and their mules heavily laden with booty. At
the spot where the drawbridge stood, the moat has been
filled up with stones, and since then the wind and the
feet of the passers-by have brought to it a little vegetable
soil into which elder-trees have forced their roots. The
walls have, to a great extent, given way; enormous fragments as big as rocks lie scattered on the ground; elsewhere stony rubbish fallen into the moat fill it half-way
up; its sides are thickly covered with chickweed. The
great court wherein formerly armed men assembled before all pillaging expeditions is encumbered with rubbish, intersected with quagmires. We hardly dare attempt to make our way through the thicket of shrubs
and tall grass; we are afraid of stepping upon some vi-
per hidden between two stones, or of falling into the
opening of some still yawning *oubliette;* let us, however, proceed, carefully picking our way. We arrive at
the edge of a well which, fortunately, is encircled with
the remains of coping-stones. Timidly we bend over the
black jaws of the chasm, and strive to sound the depth

through the hart's-tongue and bracken grown over it. We fancy that we can discern at the bottom the feeble reflection of a ray of light which has strayed into the abyss; we fancy that we hear ascending to us a sound as of a suppressed murmur. - Is it a wandering current of air eddying in the well? Is it a spring whose water oozes through the stones and trickles down drop by drop? Is it a salamander crawling about in the water, causing it to hiss—who knows? Formerly, says tradition, the confused noises issuing from these depths were the despairing cries and sobs of victims. The water of the well rests upon a bed of bones.

With an effort I turn my eyes from the chasm which fascinates me, and bring them back to the square mass of the keep, shining in broad daylight. The other towers have fallen in, this alone remains standing; it has even retained some of the battlements of its coping. The walls, grown yellow beneath the sun, are still polished as on the morrow of the day when the lord held his first feast in the great hall; hardly a crack or a scratch is to be seen; only the wood and iron work of the narrow windows set in embrasures have disappeared. In the thick walls, five yards above the ground, is an aperture which was the entrance-door; a large stone jutting out forms the threshold, and the top of the pointed arch is ornamented with rude carving bearing a curious monogram and relics of the ancient baronial device. The movable staircase which used to be attached to the threshold no longer exists, and the zealous archæologist who seeks to read, or rather to divine, the few proud words carved in the stone is obliged to have recourse to a ladder. In order to obtain access to the interior of the

tower, the peasants have made use of more violent meas-
ures—they have cut a hole in the wall on a level with
the ground.   This, no doubt, was rough treatment; but
perhaps they were animated by their thirst for vengeance
upon this keep, wherein numbers of their people had died
from starvation or torture; perhaps, also, they imagined
that they should find some hidden treasure within it.

I pass through this breach with some sense of apprehension; the air inside, to mingle with which no ray of
sun ever comes, freezes me before I have fairly entered.
Yet light descends to the bottom of the tower; the roof
has fallen in, the floors have been burned in some bygone
fire, and here and there are to be seen, half fastened into
the walls, the remains of blackened rafters.   All this
wreck of stones, wood, and cinders has become mixed up
together by degrees into a sort of paste which the waters
from the sky, descending as if into the bottom of a well,
constantly keep damp.   Sticky mud covers this soft
ground, whereon slips my foot as I venture to put it
down with a feeling of repugnance.   I seem to be imprisoned in this horrible dungeon; my only feeling is
one of disgust as I breathe this stale, mephitic air.   And
yet it is pure in comparison with that odor of decay and
bones issuing from the jagged mouth of the under-
ground dungeons.   I bend over the black hole and seek
to discern something; but I can see nothing.   I should,
indeed, have to possess sight sharpened by long obscurity
to distinguish the reflections, lost in this obscurity.   Sinister hole!   I am ignorant of the murders in which it
had been an accomplice, but I shudder with fear when I
see it; and, as if to seek strength, I look up towards the
blue sky enframed by the four great walls of the tower.

A disturbed screech-owl whirls about up above, uttering its shrill cry.

A staircase formed in the thickness of the wall enables me to climb up to the battlements. Several steps are worn away, and the staircase is thus converted into an inclined plane, most difficult to ascend; but by supporting myself by the walls, clinging to the projections, slipping into the dust only to raise myself up again, I end in reaching the coping of the tower. The stone is broad and I run no risk, yet I hardly dare move a couple of steps lest I should be overcome by dizziness, I am perched up so high, in the regions of birds and clouds, between two abysses.

On one side is the black gulf of the tower, on the other the luminous depth of the rocks and slopes lighted by the sun. The crag bearing the keep looks like another tower, several hundred yards high, and the river winding at its feet produces the effect of a mere moat of defence. Tradition tells how one of the ancient lords of the district sometimes amused himself by making his prisoners jump down from the terrace of the keep. He reserved for his most detested enemies a lingering death in the hole of the *oubliettes;* but the captives against whom he had no cause for hatred were called upon to show, when casting themselves from the tower, with what courage and good grace they could die. Of an evening these deeds would be talked over round the smoking-board; the contortions of those who recoiled in horror from the abyss would be laughed at, those applauded who with one bound had flung themselves into space. The noble lord died in a convent in the neighborhood in the "odor of sanctity."

The lowly little houses, with their roofs of slate or thatch constituting the ancient feudatory village, were irregularly clustered at the foot of the crag. What changes have been accomplished, not only in the institutions and customs, but also in the human mind, since the lord thus kept all his subjects under his eyes and feet—since the heir to his name grew up—saying to himself, of those badly clothed beings whom he saw moving about below, "If I wish it, all these men are food for my sword!" How, then, would it have been possible for even the gentlest, most gifted son of these nobles not to feel his bosom swell with fierce pride at the contemplation of all this expanse of country subject to him, of this grovelling village, these abject clods herding on the dung-heap? He might have been ready in his infancy to believe that all men have an equal right to happiness; he might have deemed himself to be born of the same clay, when one single glance over the country, from the top of the lordly terrace of his keep, would have sufficed to undeceive him. To believe in equality—not in joy, but in despair or remorse—it was necessary for him to leave his castle, to fly to the gloomy convent in some narrow valley, and to beat his brow upon the floor of some church.

In our days the descendant of these ancient cavaliers no longer requires to act as the jailer of a village, nor to watch the inhabitants with a jealous eye, unless, at least, he has become the proprietor of some works, while the villagers people his factory. The villa which he has built upon the slope of some hill-side is, so to say, kept out of sight. The nearest group of houses is marked by a curtain of big trees; and if the remote villages do peep

"AT THE CONTEMPLATION OF ALL THIS EXPANSE."

out here and there, they are but simple motives in the
landscape, features in the grand picture. The lord of
the castle is no longer the master; of what use, then,
would it be for him to give to his house a commanding
position?—solitude, in which he could enjoy nature in
peace, were better for him.

Thus, since the Middle Ages, village and castle have
ceased to constitute a world of their own; voluntarily or
compulsorily, they have entered into a larger one—into a
society in which there is more room for conflicts, in
which progress brings about a result grander in a very
different way. The little kingdom of which the lord
was absolute master is in these days but a simple district, and the descendant of the ancient barons has now
no work for his ancestor's rusty sword to do. Perhaps
he may still try to retain some of those apparent or real
privileges of his father's power which are left to him;
perhaps, while resigning himself to his rôle of subject or
citizen, he simply loses himself in the crowd. In all
cases, it is other kings and nations who have benefited
by his ancestor's fights and conquests. While they, during long years of warfare against the mountaineers, had
succeeded in forcing the latter into their retreats, oblig-
ing them to remove the frontier of their domains to the
snowy crests, in their turn they have had to receive the
visit of some invader, and the limit which they had set
to their possessions became lost in the vast circumference of a powerful empire.

A curious name which is to be met with in many parts
of the mountains caused me to dream of things of the
past. In a ravine, merely a slight dip in the ground, a
spring, which would hardly be visible did not a ray of

the sun reveal its existence, gleams from afar like a little
sparkling diamond. I draw near, the leaves of the water-
cress alternately bend and rise up again beneath the silvery drops passing over them ; birds flutter round me,
and the plant, bathing its roots in the hidden water,
darts its green stems and flowers out far above the with-
ered turf of the pastures. This little patch of verdure,
which the shepherds see from afar upon the gray burnt-
up-looking face of the mountain slopes, is the " Fountain
of the Three Lords."

Why this strange title ? How could so trivial a spring
have thus assumed the name of three potentates ? The
legend of the mountains tells us that at a very ancient
period, in the times when strong castles surrounded with
moats rose up on all the crags of the defiles, three
counts, who chanced not to be at war, went out hunting
in the vicinity of the little fountain. They were weary
with their long chase in pursuit of wild boars and stags,
and the sweat ran down their brows. Their crowd of
servitors pressed round them, vying with one another in
offering them wine and metheglin ; but the tiny thread
of water trickling through the fissure of the rock seemed
a more agreeable beverage than any of the liquors poured
into silver goblets. One after another they bent over the
little basin of the spring, pushed aside with their hands
the weeds floating on the surface of the water, and drank
as if simple shepherds or fawns from the mountains.
Then they looked at one another, held out the hand of
friendship, and, lying down on the grass, began to chat
merrily. The weather was fine ; the sun had already descended low on the horizon ; some scattered clouds cast
long shadows upon the ripening cornfields in the plains ;

here and there delicate smoke curled up from the villages. The three companions felt in a good humor. Until then their vast domains in the mountain had had no precise limits; they decided that henceforth the spring whose icy thread of water had allayed their thirst should be the point of separation for the three counties. The one was to follow the right, the other the left bank of the streamlet; the third should occupy the whole of the brow of the hill extending from the source to the neighboring summit, and from there to the opposite side. In testimony of the treaty just concluded, the three lords filled their hands with several little drops from the fountain, and each sprinkled them over the turf of his domain.

But, alas! those beautiful days are not to last, and the noble counts are not always smiling or good friends. The three comrades quarrelled; war broke out. Vassals, burghers, and peasants cut each other's throats in the forests and ravines, with a view to removing the boundaries of the three counties. The plain was devastated, and for several generations torrents of blood flowed for the sake of the possession of that drop of water trickling up above upon the peaceful heights. At last peace is made; and if war commence again, it will not now be among the three barons, nor for the conquest of a simple fountain, but between puissant sovereigns, and for the possession of immense territories, containing mountains, forests, rivers, and populous towns. They are no longer badly armed bands massacring one another; they are hundreds of thousands of men provided with the most scientific means of destruction, who fling themselves upon and kill each other. There is no doubt that humanity does progress, but at the sight of these terrible conflicts one is sometimes led to doubt it.

How happy, then, it would appear, must be those retired populations in the loftily situated valleys who have never to suffer warfare, or who, at least, in spite of the flux and reflux of armies on the march, have ended in preserving their pristine independence! Many races of mountaineers, protected by their enormous groups of mountains joined together, have experienced this good-fortune of remaining free. They know that it is not merely to the heroism of their hearts, to the strength of their arms, to the unity of their purpose, that they owe the bliss never to have been subdued by powerful neighbors. It is also to their great Alps that they must return thanks; these are the steadfast columns which have defended the entrance to their temple.

Chapter XVIII.

CRETINS.

By the side of these strong, valiant men, with their stout chests, their piercing glance, who climb the rocks with steady steps, hideous masses of living flesh drag themselves along; they are cretins, with drooping goitres. Yet among these masses are many who cannot even do so much; there they sit upon filthy chairs, swinging their bodies and heads from side to side, allowing the saliva to run down their dirty rags. These creatures cannot walk; there are some who have not even been able to acquire the art of carrying their food to their mouths: they are fed with pap until they are surfeited, and when they feel the soft nourishment slip down into their stomachs they utter a little grunt of satisfaction. Such are the last representatives of that humankind "whose countenances were created to look upon the stars." What a wide distance lies between Apollo of Pythion's ideal head and that of the poor cretin, with his sightless eyes and his distorted grimaces! Much more beautiful is the reptile's head, for it resembles its own type, and we do not expect to see it different, while the face of the idiot is a hideously degenerate form; we see from afar what seems to us to be a man, and the intelligence of the beast is not even displayed upon those discordant features!

As a climax of horror, the rudimentary sentiments revealed in this unhappy creature are not always good. Some cretins are malevolent. These grind their teeth, utter fierce roars, make angry gesticulations with their clumsy arms; they stamp upon the ground, and, if they were left alone, would devour the flesh and drink the blood of those who tend them so devotedly. What matters this rage to the simple and good mountaineers? In spite of it, they have given to the poor idiots the names of "cretins," "créstias," or "innocents," in the belief that these creatures, incapable of reasoning about their actions and of arriving at the comprehension of evil, enjoy the privilege of bearing no sin upon their conscience. Christians from their cradle, they could not fail to go straight to heaven. It is thus that in Mussulman countries the crowd prostrates itself before madmen and monomaniacs, and glories in being touched by their spittle or excrements. Since, in their human form, they live without the pale of humanity, there can be no doubt that they constitute a divine dream!

Yet among these unfortunates there are some who are really good, who love to do their best in their narrow circle. One day I had gone down into the valley to ascend by the other side to a plateau of pastures, in the midst of which I had seen from afar the waters of a small lake. Without stopping, I had passed a little damp hut, surrounded by some alders, and leisurely pursued a path faintly marked by animals' feet, at the side of a rapid stream. I had already gone more than a stone's-throw beyond the hut when I heard behind me a heavy, hurried step; at the same time, stertorous, almost rattling, breathing proceeded from the creature pursuing and gaining upon me. I turned round and saw a poor cretin, whose goitre, shaken by the chase, swayed heavily from shoulder to shoulder. I had great difficulty in restraining an ejaculation of horror, on seeing this human mass advancing towards me, throwing herself alternately first on one leg and then on the other. The monster made a sign to me to wait, then stopped before me, looking fixedly at me with vacant eyes, and puffing her rattling breath into my face. With a warning gesture, she pointed to the defile into which I was about to enter, then joined her hands to show me that sharp rocks barred the passage. "There, there!" she uttered, indicating a more distinctly marked-out footpath, rising as it winds up the incline and reaches a plateau by which it goes round the impassable defile in the bottom. When she saw me follow her good advice and begin to climb the slope, she uttered two or three grunts of satisfaction, followed me with her eyes for some time, then retired quietly, happy to have performed a good action. I confess I felt that I was humiliated rather than she. A creature afflicted by nature, horrible, a kind of thing without form and without name, had not rested until she had saved me from a wrong step; and I, a proud man—I, who knew myself to be endowed by nature with a certain amount of reason, and who had reached the sense of moral responsibility—how many times had I not, without saying a word, allowed other men, and even those whom I called my friends, to enter upon much more formidable paths than a defile in the mountains! The idiot, the goitrous woman, had taught me my duty. Thus, even in what appeared to me to be lower than humanity, I found that benevolence so often lacking in those who think them-

selves great and strong.   No creature is too low to fall
beneath love, and even respect.   Who, then, is right—
the ancient Spartan, who threw all malformed children
into a chasm, or the mother who, while weeping, suckles
and caresses her idiot, deformed son?   Certainly we cannot say that the mothers are wrong who struggle against
all hope to rescue their children from death; but society
must come to the assistance of these unfortunates, with
science and affection to cure those who are curable, to
give all happiness possible to those whose condition is
hopeless, and to do its utmost, that hygienic practice and
the comprehension of physiological laws may more and
more reduce the number of similar births.

A regular course of education can refine these dull
natures; and when a mother's affection is followed up by
the solicitude of a companion who succeeds in teaching
the poor innocent to accomplish some rude task, he by
degrees becomes developed, and ends by showing something like a gleam of intelligence upon his face.   Among
the innumerable pictures graven in my memory while
crossing the mountain, I discover one which still, after
long years, touches and moves me.   It was evening, towards one of the latter days in summer.   The meadows in
the valley were mown a second time, and here and there
I perceived little haycocks whose sweet scent was wafted
to me by the breeze.   I was walking along a winding
path, enjoying the freshness of the evening, the perfume
of the plants, the beauty of the peaks lighted up by the
declining sun.   Suddenly, at a turn in the road, I found
myself in the presence of a singular group.   A goitred
cretin was harnessed by cords to a species of cart filled
with hay.   Without any difficulty he drew the heavy ve-

"WITH HIM THE LAD FORMED A YOKE."

hicle, seeing neither bogs nor the great scattered blocks,
and pulling as if with blind force. But by his side was
his little brother, a pretty, active child with an intelligent
smiling face; it was he who saw and thought for the
monster. By a sign, a touch, he made his brother incline
to the right or the left to avoid obstacles, hastening or
slackening his speed; with him the lad formed a yoke,
of which he was the mind and the other the body. As
they passed, the boy greeted me with a pleasant gesture,
and pushing Caliban with his elbow, made him remove
his cap and turn his soulless eyes towards me. Yet I
seemed to see something in them like a gleam of a human
sentiment of respect and friendship; and I, with a feeling of reverence, greeted this touching group, this symbol of humankind.

Left to himself, and rejoicing merely in the instinctive
lights of an animal, the cretin can sometimes accomplish
things which would be above the power of an intelligent
man filled with the consciousness of his own importance.
Frequently my companion the shepherd had related to
me the story of a fall he had met with down a crevasse in
the glacier; and when he spoke of it, horror would still
be depicted upon his face. He was sitting upon the talus,
close to the edge of a glacier, when a stone, in falling,
caused him to lose his balance, and, without being able
to stop himself, he slipped into a yawning chasm opening out between the rock and the compact mass of the
ice; suddenly he found himself as if at the bottom of a
well, hardly able to perceive one ray of light from the
skies. He was stunned, contused, but none of his limbs
were broken. Impelled by the instinct of self-preserva-
tion, he managed to cling to the walls of the rock and to

climb up from projection to projection, until within a
few yards of the aperture; there he beheld the sun once
more, the pastures, the sheep, and his dog, who was watching him with fervent eyes.   But, having reached this
ledge, the shepherd could climb no farther; above, the
rock was smooth on every side, leaving nothing for his
hand to grip.   The animal was as desperate as his master; he flung himself from side to side, upon the edge of
the precipice; he gave vent to several short barks, then
suddenly sped off like a dart in the direction of the valley.   The shepherd had nothing more to fear.   He knew
that the good dog was gone in search of help, and that
he would soon return accompanied by shepherds with
ropes.   Nevertheless, during the period of suspense he
passed through horrible agonies of despair; he felt as if
the faithful brute would never return; he saw himself
dying of hunger upon his rock, and asked himself with
horror if the eagles would not come to tear morsels of
flesh from his limbs before he was quite dead.   And yet
he recollected perfectly how, in a similar case, an "innocent" had behaved.   Having fallen to the bottom of a
crevasse, whence it was impossible for him to ascend, the
cretin had not exhausted himself with useless efforts;
he waited patiently, beating his feet upon the ground so
as to keep up animal warmth, and thus waited patiently
through a whole evening, a whole night, then through
half of the following day.   At last having heard his
name shouted by those in search of him, he responded,
and soon after was drawn up out of the gulf.   His only
complaint was that he had been very cold.

But whatever, alas! may be the privileges and immu-
nities of the cretin, even although the unfortunate creat-

ure has no need to fear the cares and deceptions of the man who carves out his own path in life, it is not the less necessary to strive to wrest the cretin out of his " innocence " and his disgusting maladies, in order to give him, at the same time as physical strength, a sense of his own moral responsibility. He must be made to enter into the companionship of free men; and to cure and elevate him it is necessary first to know what have been the causes of his degeneracy. Learned men, **bending over** their retorts and books, offer opposite opinions; some **say that** the deformity of the goitre proceeds principally from the want of iodine in the drinking-water, and that by interbreeding moral deformity ends in being added to that of **the** body; the others rather believe that goitre and cretinism are produced by the water, which, descended from the snow, has not had time to be sufficiently stirred and aerated before it reaches the village, or else by having passed over rocks containing magnesia. It is certain that bad water can frequently contribute to **germinating and** developing disease; but is **that** all?

It is enough to enter one of those cabins in which the idiots are born and vegetate to see that there exist other causes for their lamentable position. The habitation is gloomy and smoky; the chests, the table, the rafters, are worm-eaten; in corners into which our eyes cannot thoroughly penetrate **we** perceive indistinct forms covered with filth and spiders' webs. The earth which does duty for a floor is left constantly damp, and as if viscous from all the rubbish and impure **water** covering it. The air breathed in that confined space is foul and fetid. Sometimes the odors of smoke, rancid lard, mouldy bread, worm-eaten wood, dirty linen, human emanations, can all

be simultaneously perceived. At night every aperture
is closed to prevent the cold from without penetrating
into the chamber; grandparents, father, mother, children,
all sleep in a sort of shelved cupboard, whose curtains are
closed by day, where during the night's slumber a dense
air accumulates, far more impure even than that in the
rest of the cabin. Nor is this all; during the cold of the
winter, the family, in order to keep themselves warmer,
migrate from the ground-floor and descend into the cellar,
which at the same time serves for a stable. On one side
are the animals, lying on dirty straw; on the other the
men and women, sleeping beneath their grimy sheets. A
gutter separates the two groups of vertebrate mammals,
but the air breathed is common to all. Nor, again, can
this air, penetrating through narrow chinks, be renewed
for many weeks, on account of the snow covering the
ground; it is necessary to dig out a sort of chimney
through which nothing but a wan ray of light descends.
In these cellars day itself resembles a polar night.

   Is it astonishing that in such dwellings, scrofulous,
rickety, deformed children should be born? From the
first week numberless newly born babes are shaken by
terrible convulsions, to which the greatest portion suc-
cumb; in certain countries mothers are so used to the
death of their children that they hardly consider them to
be alive until the formidable passage of the "five days'
malady" has been gone through. And how many of
those who do escape live anything but a life of sickness
and insanity? Excellent as the surrounding air of the
free mountain and the outdoor work are for developing
a sound man's strength and agility, so, in proportion, do
the confined space and humid gloom of the cabin con-

tribute to render worse the condition of the cretin and the goitrous victim. By the side of the one brother who becomes the handsomest and strongest among the young people, another brother drags himself along, a sort of fearful, living, fleshy **excrescence!**

In many localities, people have already begun to build asylums for these unfortunates. Nothing is wanting in those modern abodes. Pure air circulates freely through them, the sun lights **up every** room, the water is pure and wholesome, all the furniture, and especially the beds, are exquisitely clean, the "innocents" have attendants who look after them as would nurses, and professors who strive to cause **a ray** of intellectual light to enter into their impenetrable brains. Frequently they succeed, and the cretin may gradually awaken to a superior life. But it is not of so much importance to labor at repairing an evil which has already occurred as it is to guard against it. These infected hovels, so picturesque sometimes in the landscape, must disappear to make room for commodious, healthy houses; air and light must enter freely into every habitation of man; sound bodily health as well as perfect moral dignity must be observed everywhere. At this price the mountaineers will in a few generations purchase complete immunity from all those maladies which now degrade so great a number among them. Then the inhabitants will be worthy of the country surrounding them; they will be able with satisfaction to contemplate the lofty snow-clad summits, and to say, with the ancient Greeks, "These are our ancestors, and **we** resemble them."

CHAPTER XIX.

MOUNTAIN-WORSHIP.

THE worship of nature still exists in the world to an almost incredible extent. How often has a peasant, uncovering his head, pointed to the sun, and solemnly said to me, " There is our god !" And even I—shall I confess it?—have many a time been impelled by real feeling, at sight of lofty eminences, enthroned above valleys and plains, to call them divine.

One day I was laboriously making my way up a narrow pass, very steep, and obstructed by rolling stones. The wind poured down the pass, and beat upon me, with blinding dashes of rain and sleet; a gray veil of mist hid the rocks from my sight, but here and there, in the obscurity, I caught glimpses of black and threatening masses, which seemed by turn to retire and to approach me, according as the fog was more or less dense. I was benumbed, depressed, miserable. All at once a gleam of light, reflected by the countless particles of water in the air, caused me to look upwards. Above my head the cloud of water and snow had parted; the blue sky was beaming upon me, and high up in this clear azure appeared the serene brow of a mountain : its snowy covering, embroidered by sharp points of rock, as if with fine arabesques, shone with the brilliancy of silver, and the sun edged it with a line of gold. The outlines of the mountain were true and precise, like those of a statue standing resplendent in a background of darkness ; but the superb pyramid seemed to be absolutely detached from earth : tranquil, strong, unchangeable in its repose, it appeared to hang suspended in the sky, and to belong to another world than this heavy planet, all wrapped in clouds and fogs. In this apparition I thought I saw something more than the valley of happiness — more, even, than Olympus, the abode of the gods. But a vicious cloud came suddenly, and closed the opening through which I had beheld the mountain : I found myself once more in the wind, the mist and rain, but I consoled myself with the thought, "a divine revelation has appeared to me."

In the earliest historic times, all people had this feeling in regard to mountains : they saw in them divinities, or, at least, the throne of superior beings, alternately visible and hidden under a passing veil of clouds. It was to these mountains they ascribed, generally, the origin of their race ; in them they fixed the seat of their traditions or legends ; to them they looked as the scene where their ambitions and their dreams would be realized in the future; and it was always from them their saviour, the angel of glory or liberty, was expected to come down. So important a part have lofty mountain-peaks always borne in the life of nations that one might almost tell the history of humanity by that of mountain-worship; they are like great milestones set here and there on the march of advancing races.

It was in the valleys between the great mountains of Central Asia, according to learned scholars, that those of

our ancestors to whom we owe our European languages
established themselves in civilized tribes, the first that
were ever known; and at the southern base of the highest mountain range in the world live the Hindoos, that
Aryan race whose ancient civilization comes down to
them as a sort of ennobling birthright. Their ancient
songs tell us with what pious fervor they celebrated
their "eighty-four thousand mountains of gold," which
rear themselves heavenward in the light beyond the
plains and forests. To the inhabitants of that region
the grand mountains of Himalaya—with their snow-clad
summits, their great glaciers—are gods themselves, glo-
rying in their power and majesty. The Gaurisankar,
whose peak pierces the sky, and the Chamalari, not so
high, but more colossal in appearance, by reason of its
isolation, are doubly worshipped as the great goddess
united to the great god; their ice-fields are a bed of
crystals and diamonds; the purple and gold clouds are
the sacred veil which enwraps them. There, above, is
the god Siva, who destroys and creates; there, also, is
the goddess Chama, the Gauri, who conceives and produces; from her are descended plants, rivers, animals,
and mankind.

In this wonderful growth of epic poetry and tradition
have taken root many other legends relating to the mountains of Himalaya, all of which represent them as living
a sublime life, either as goddesses or as the mothers of
continents and nations. Such is the poetic legend which
pictures the habitable earth as a great lotus-flower, whose
leaves are the peninsulas spread out upon the ocean, and
whose stamens and pistils are the mountains of Merou,
the springs of all life. The glaciers, the torrents and

rivers which bring down enriching soil from above, are also living beings, gods and goddesses of a lower rank, who place the humble mortals of the plains in indirect communication with the superior divinities sitting above in luminous space.

Not only Mount Merou, the culminating point of the planet, but all the other ranges, all the mountain heights of India, were worshipped by the peoples who dwelt on their sides and at their base. Mounts Vindhya, **Satpurah**, Aravulli, Neilgherry, had all their worshippers. **In** the flat countries, where the faithful had no mountains **to look at,** they built themselves temples, which, with their rows of unshapely pyramids of huge blocks of granite, represented the venerated heights of Mount Merou. Perhaps it was a similar sentiment of awe for great elevations which led the ancient Egyptians **to** construct the pyramids, those artificial mountains reared upon a foundation of sand and clay.

The Island of Ceylon, Lanka, "the resplendent," that happy spot where, according to an Eastern legend, the first of our race were sent, by divine mercy, after their expulsion from Paradise, also has its sacred mountains. Such, among others, is Mihintala, an isolated peak in the middle of a plain, with its sacred city of Anarajapura. It was on the rocky summit of Mihintala that the Hindoo missionary Mahindo alighted, twenty-two centuries ago, after his flight from the banks of the Ganges, to convert the Cingalese to the religion of Buddha. A temple now marks the spot where the saint descended; and though it is an immense edifice, the pious zeal of the pilgrims is so great that they have often covered it entirely, from base to dome, with a mantle of flowers.

A blazing carbuncle glitters at the pinnacle of the temple, flashing back from afar the rays of the sun.   Formerly a rajah caused a great carpet, six miles in length, to be spread from the top of the mountain to the plain below, so that the feet of the faithful might not touch the impure dust from unconsecrated earth.

And yet the fame of this sacred mountain Mihintala pales in comparison with the celebrated Adam's Peak, which is visible far out at sea to sailors approaching the Island of Ceylon.   The impress of a gigantic foot, belonging, apparently, to a man ten yards high, is hollowed into the rock at the extremity of the peak.   This footprint, say the Mohammedans and Jews, is that of the first man, Adam, who ascended the mountain to get a view of the earth, the vast forests, the mountains and plains, the shores and great ocean, with its islands and its dangers.   According to the Cingalese and Indians, this is not the footprint of a man at all, but of a god, who has left this trace of his presence.   This reigning deity, the Brahmins tell us, was Siva; the Buddhists say he was Buddha; while the Gnostics of the early Christian period call him Jehovah.   When the conquering Portuguese landed on the Island of Ceylon, they, so to speak, degraded the mountain, which, in their opinion, did not at all compare with the Holy Land; in the mysterious footprint they saw nothing more remarkable than a trace of St. Thomas, or, perhaps, of the Eunuch of Candace, an ancient missionary and second-rate apostle.   Moses Chorenensis, an Armenian, jealous of the claim of his own noble Mount Ararat, was still less respectful, and saw on the top of Adam's Peak only the footprints of Satan, the eternal enemy.   Finally, the

English travellers who, more and more each year, made the ascent of the holy mountain, saw in the "divine imprint" only an ordinary cavity in the rock, enlarged and rudely carved into shape. You can imagine with what contempt these strangers are regarded by the faithful who come to prostrate themselves on the rock, devoutly kiss the footprint, and place their offerings in the house of the priest. To them everything bears testimony to the authenticity of the miracle. At a point some yards below the summit a small spring flows from the **rock**: it was the staff of the deity that caused it to issue forth; **numbers of** trees grow upon the mountain-side, and **these trees, they** say, incline all their branches towards the summit, to blossom and grow in the act of worship.

The rocks on the mountain are strewn with precious stones: these are the **tears** which have fallen from the eyes of the deity at sight of the crimes and sufferings of mankind. How could they fail to believe in the miracle, in view of all these riches, which suggested the tales of the "Thousand and One Nights?" The streamlets which flow from the mountain do not wash down common pebbles and sand, like our streams; they bring with them a deposit of **rubies** and sapphires and garnets, and the bather who disports himself in their waters wallows, like the sirens, in a bed of precious stones.

Those **races of the** extreme East, whose civilization has followed a different course from that of the Aryan race, have worshipped their mountains with the same **fervor**. In China and Japan, as well as in India, the mountain-tops are crowned with temples consecrated to the gods, when they are not themselves regarded as tutelary or avenging deities; and to these divine moun-

tains the people try to connect their history by legends
and traditions.

The most ancient historic mountains are those of China, for the people of the "middle race" were among the
first to arrive at a knowledge of themselves, and the first
to write down their connected history. Their sacred
mountains, five in number, are all in districts famous
for their agriculture, their industries, their dense population, and the remarkable events which have occurred
near by. The most sacred of these mountains, the Taï-
Chan, overtops all the other heights in the rich penin-
sula of Chan-Toung, between the two gulfs of the Yellow Sea. From the top, which one reaches by a paved
road and steps hewn in the solid rock, one sees stretched
at its feet the rich plains which the Hoang-Ho crosses
as it goes winding about between the two gulfs, supplying water to multitudes of people more numerous than
the leaves of the forest. The Emperor Choung made
the ascent four hundred and thirty years ago, so the history of the country records. Confucius, also, tried to
climb to the top, but the ascent is difficult; the philoso-
pher stopped short, and the spot is still pointed out where
he turned back. All the superior gods and the principal
genii have their temples and altars on this sacred mountain, and so, likewise, have the clouds, the sky, the Great
Bear, and the Polar Star.

Here the ten thousand genii pause in their flight to
contemplate the earth and the cities of mankind. "The
honor of Taï-Chan equals that of heaven: it controls the
world; it collects the clouds and sends us rain; it decides
upon births and deaths, upon good and bad fortune,
honor and disgrace. Of all the peaks which touch the

sky, none is worthier of a visit." And so pilgrims flock there in crowds to pray for all mercies; and the way is lined with caves where beggars with hideous sores lie in wait, a horror to passers-by.

The Japanese, with more reason than the Chinese—for their volcanic mountains are wonderfully beautiful—look upon their snow-clad summits with adoration. Is there any idol in the world could rival their magnificent Fusi-Yama, the "mountain beyond compare," which rises almost isolated in the middle of a plain, its base covered with forests, its sides with snow? Formerly the volcano poured forth smoke, and seethed with flame and lava; now it is silent, but in the Archipelago there are several volcanic mountains which still emit rivers of fire upon the trembling earth.

Among these mountains there is one, the most terrible of all, which people thought to appease by throwing into the crater thousands of Christians as an offering. In the same way, in the New World, they tried to calm Mount Monotombo by casting into it the priests who had dared to preach against it, declaring it was not a god, but the mouth of hell. On the other hand, volcanoes do not generally wait for victims to be thrown into their craters; they know only too well how to lay hold of them when they rend the earth, pour down lakes of mud, and cover whole provinces with ashes: at one stroke they destroy the inhabitants of an entire country. Is not this enough to inspire worship in the minds of those who bow their heads before power? The volcano destroys; therefore it is a god.

So mountain-worship, like all other religions, takes possession of man through various instincts in his nature.

At the foot of a volcano ejecting lava, it is terror which makes him bow his face to the ground; in the parched fields, it is need of help that makes him look appealingly to the snowy mountains, the source of streams; gratitude, also, has made worshippers of many who have found a safe refuge in the valley or on the rugged mountain-side; finally, admiration would inspire religious feeling in all men, in proportion as the love of the beautiful was developed in them. What mountain is there that has not its beautiful scenery and its safe place of refuge, and which is not either terrible or beneficent—generally both together? Wandering tribes can easily connect all their traditions with any mountain which happens to be upon their horizon, and bring their religion to it; so at each stage in their long journeys a new temple erects itself. Formerly the wandering tribes on the plains of Persia towards evening always saw a mountain rising up from the middle of the sandy plain: it was Mount Telesme, the holy "talisman," which followed its worshippers in their wanderings about the world; and when, after a long journey, the mountain seen from afar proved to be not a deceptive image, but a real height with its snows and rocks, who could then doubt that their god had made the journey to accompany his people?

In the same way, the mountain on whose top the fugitives from the Deluge landed has never ceased moving about from place to place. A Samaritan version of the Pentateuch asserts that Adam's Peak is the point on which Noah's ark came to anchor; other versions declare that Ararat is the real mountain; but which Ararat is it?—the one in Armenia, or quite a different one on which the priests have found remains of the sacred ship? In every part of the East the people claim this honor for their own special mountain, whose waters irrigate their lands: that, they say, is the mountain from which the stream of life came back to earth, following the course of the snows and brooks. Proofs are by no means wanting to sustain all these traditions: have they not found pieces of petrified wood, even under the glaciers? and in the rocks themselves, have they not discovered traces of those "rings of the Deluge" which our modern scientists call ammonite fossils?

Besides these, more than a hundred mountains in Persia, Syria, Arabia, and Asia Minor claim to be the landing-place of the patriarch, second father of the human race. Greece also points to her Parnassus, from which the stones were thrown upon the ground, after the Deluge, and became men. Even in France there are mountains where the ark is said to have anchored: one of these sacred heights is Chamechande, near the Grande Chartreuse of Grenoble; another is the Puy de Prigue, above the sources of the Aude.

The myth has the merit of consistency; men have always descended from high elevations: it is also from a lofty eminence, the throne of the Deity, that the great Voice is heard declaring their duty to mortals. The God of the Jews sat on the summit of Mount Sinai amid clouds and lightnings, and spoke with the voice of thunder to the people assembled on the plain. In the same way Baal, Moloch—all the sanguinary gods of those Oriental races—appeared to their faithful on the tops of mountains. In Arabia Petræa, in the land of Edom and Moab, there is not a mountain height, not a hill, not a rock, which does not possess its great pyramid of stones, the altar on which priests have sacrificed blood to propitiate the Deity. At Babel, where there was no mountain, they substituted that famous temple which was designed to touch the heavens. The poet has restored this giant edifice, not as it was, but as the people pictured it:

> " Each of the largest mountains with its granite sides
> Would furnish but one stone."

In their jealous hatred of foreign religions, the Jewish prophets often cursed the "high-places," on which their neighbors set their idols; but they themselves did not act differently, and it was to the mountains that they looked, thence to evoke their succoring angels. Their temple was erected upon a mountain, and upon a mountain was it that Elijah conversed with God. When the Galilean was transfigured and floated in uncreated light with the two prophets, Moses and Elijah, it was from Mount Tabor that He ascended. When He died between two thieves, it was upon the summit of a mountain that he was crucified; and when He shall come again, says the prophecy—when He shall come again, surrounded by saints and angels, and shall take part in the punishment of His enemies, it is upon a mountain that He shall descend, which one touch of His foot will suffice to break. Another mountain, an ideal summit bearing a new city of gold and diamonds, will spring up in the luminous space, and it is there that the chosen will live for evermore, far above this world of weariness and woe.

Chapter XX.

OLYMPUS AND THE GODS.

JUST as the glory of invisible **Greece surpasses** in brilliancy **that of all** other empires **of** the East, **so has** Olympus, the loftiest, **most beautiful of the** Hellenes' **sacred** mountains, become in people's imaginations the mountain *par excellence;* no other peaks, not those of **Merou, of Elburz, of Ararat, nor** of Lebanon, awaken in the minds of men the same memories **of** grandeur and majesty. And few, indeed, were so admirably **and conspicuously** situated, or served so well as **a** beacon to the races overrunning the world. **Placed in an angle of** the Ægean Sea, and by fully half its height overtopping all the neighboring summits, Olympus can be perceived **by** sailors from enormous **distances.** From the plains of Macedonia, **from** the rich valleys of Thessaly, from **the** mountains Othrys, **Pindus,** Bermius, Athos, its triple dome, and its slopes with the "thousand folds" of which Homer speaks, can be distinguished on the horizon. The fertility of the country extended at its feet attracted populations from every part, who **met there to** mingle and amalgamate in various ways, or mutually to destroy one another. **Finally,** Olympus commands the defiles which the tribes or **armies on** the march from Asia into Europe, **or from Greece to the barbarous countries** of the north,

were obliged to pass through; it rises up like a milestone
upon the great highway then pursued by nations.

Several other mountains of the Hellenic world owed
to their sparkling snow the name Olympus, or the "luminous;" but none better merited it than that of Thessaly, whose summit served as a throne for the gods.   It
was in the plains and valleys extended beneath the shadow of the great mountain that the people of Hellas had
passed its national infancy.   It was from Thessaly that
came the Hellenes of Attica and the Peloponnesus; it
was there that their first heroes had done battle with
monsters, and that their first poets, guided by the voice
of the Pierides, had composed hymns and songs of gladness and victory.   While flocking towards distant lands,
the Greek tribes never forgot the divine mountain which
had produced and nourished them in its dales.

Almost every great event of mythical history was accomplished in that portion of Greece; the most important among them being the struggle which decided between the sovereignty of the heavens and the earth.
Olympus was the citadel chosen by the new gods, and
on every side were encamped those ancient deities, the
monstrous Titans, sons of Chaos.   Standing upon the
mountains of Othrys, the giants seized enormous rocks,
whole mountains, and hurled them against half-uprooted
Olympus.   That they might rise still higher towards
the sky, the old Titans piled mountain upon mountain,
forming a pedestal for themselves, but the great snowy
summit always overtopped them; it surrounded itself
with dark thunder-belching clouds.   Supplied with the
same powers by the earth, the giants' voices were filled
with the roaring of the storms, their arms with the vigor

of the tempest; with their hundred arms they hurled at random their hail-storm of rocks; but they were fighting with the blind fury of the elements when pitted against the young intelligent gods. They succumbed, and beneath the ruins of the mountain entire nations were crushed with them. It is thus that the caprices of kings have often caused nations to be massacred as if inadvertently.

Many generations had passed away since these prodigious conflicts of Olympus, ere the Ionic and Doric tribes first possessed poets to sing their exploits, and subsequently historians to recount them. Then Zeus, the father of gods and men, sat in peace upon the sacred mountain; his throne was placed upon the highest peak; by his side was the goddess Here, virgin and matron; around him were placed the immortals, with their eternally beautiful and glad countenances. A luminous atmosphere bathed the summit of Olympus and played amid the locks of the gods; never did tempests come to trouble the repose of these happy beings; nor rain nor snow fell upon the radiant summit. The clouds collected by Zeus were unrolled at his feet around the rocks forming the magnificent base of his throne. Through the interstices of this veil, which the Horæ opened and shut according to their master's will, the latter looked down upon the earth and sea, the cities and their inhabitants.

He held inflexible destinies suspended above the heads of these struggling men; he decreed life or death, distributed beneficent rain or vengeful thunder, according to his caprice. No lamentation ascending from below disturbed the gods in their eternal quiet. Their nectar was ever delicious, their ambrosia always exquisite. They inhaled with relish the odor of hecatombs; lis-

tened, as if to music, to the concert of suppliant voices.
Beneath them was unrolled, like an endless picture, the
spectacle of struggles and of human miseries : they beheld
armies dash against one another, fleets become ingulfed,
towns disappear amid flames and smoke, the poor toilers
(almost invisible myrmidons) exhausting themselves in
efforts to gather in harvests of which a master should
despoil them ; even beneath the roofs of the dwellings
they saw women weeping and children wailing.   Afar
off their enemy, Prometheus, was dying upon a rock of
Mount Caucasus.   Such were the pleasures of the gods.

Did ever a Hellene, shepherd, priest, or king, dare to
climb up the slopes of Olympus, away above the lofty
pastures of its dales and crests?   Did even one only
venture by placing his foot upon the great peak, to find
himself suddenly in the presence of these terrible gods?
Ancient writers tell us that philosophers are not afraid
of scaling Mount Etna, although much higher than Olympus; but they never mention one single mortal who has
had the temerity to ascend the mountain of the gods,
not even in the days of science, in that age when philosophers taught that Zeus and the other immortals were
mere conceptions of the human mind.

Later on, other religions, disseminated among the various people living in the surrounding plains, took possession of the sacred mountain and consecrated it to new
divinities.   There the Greek Christians worshipped the
Holy Trinity instead of Zeus; they still look upon its
three principal peaks as the three great thrones of heav-
en.   One of its loftiest points, which formerly perhaps
bore a temple of Apollo, is now surmounted by a mon-
astery of St. Elias ; one of its dales, wherein the Bac-

chantes were wont to sing *Evoë!* in honor of Dionysos or Bacchus, is inhabited by the monks of St. Denys. Priests have succeeded to priests, and the superstitious respect of modern times to the worship of the ancient; but perhaps the highest summit is yet untrodden by human steps; the soft light, resplendent above its rocks and snow, has not beamed upon any man since the Hellenic gods took their departure.

A few years ago it would have been difficult for a European to attain the summit of the mountain, for the Hellenic *klephtes*, unerring shots, occupied all its gorges; they had entrenched themselves in it, as within an enormous citadel, and thence, recommencing the conflict of the gods against the Titans, they set out upon their expeditions against the Turks of Mount Ossa. Proud of their courage, they believed themselves as invincible as the mountain upon which they lived; they endowed Olympus itself with life.. "I am," said one of their songs—"I am Olympus, illustrious in all ages, and renowned amid nations; forty-two peaks bristle upon my brow; seventy-two fountains flow down my ravines, and an eagle is perched upon my highest summit bearing in its claws the head of a valiant hero!" This eagle, no doubt, was that of ancient Zeus. Even nowadays he feeds on man, by man destroyed.

People's imagination knows no limits concerning the gods it has created. In the course of centuries it has changed their names, their attributes, and their powers, according to the alternations of history, the changes of languages, the individual and national variations of traditions; finally, it has caused them to die, as it gave them birth, and has replaced them by new divinities.

9*

It thus costs them but little to make their journey from mountain to mountain. Each summit, too, possessed its own god or even its Pleiades of celestial beings. Zeus dwelt upon Mount Ida just as he did upon the Olympus of Greece, upon that of Crete, of Cyprus, and upon the rocks of the Ægina; Apollo had his dwelling upon Parnassus and Helicon, upon Cyllene and Taygetus, upon all the scattered mountains rising out of the Ægean Sea. The peaks, gilded by the rays of dawning day, when the lower plains still lay in shadow, were to be consecrated to the god of the sun. And almost all the isolated summits of Hellas at the present day bear the name of Elias. The Jewish prophet, by virtue of his name, has thus become the heir of Helios, son of Jupiter.

"Behold this throne, the centre of the earth," said Æschylus, in speaking of Delphos. This central pillar rose up in many another place, according to the poet's fancy or popular imagination. Pindar beheld it in Etna; the sailors from the Archipelago pointed out Mount Athos, that great landmark which could always be discerned above the waters, whether on quitting the shores of Asia or while sailing on the seas of Europe. So lofty is this mountain that upon it the sun is said to go to rest three hours later than in the plains at its feet; it can overlook the most distant confines of the earth. When Hellas, formerly free, was subjugated by the Macedonian, when it became the slave of a master, it found a flatterer vile enough, a man sycophantish enough, to implore Alexander, who had decreed that he should be proclaimed a god, to employ an army to transform Mount Athos into a statue of the new son of Zeus, "more powerful than his father."

This impossible task might have tempted an upstart god, who was mad with pride; yet even Alexander dared not undertake it. The mariners sailing at the foot of the great mountain continued to look upon it as an ancient deity until the day whereon began another cycle in history, bringing with it a new religion and new divinities. Then people told how Mount Athos was the very mountain to which the devil transported Jesus the Galilean, to show him all the kingdoms of the earth lying outstretched at his feet—Europe, Asia, and the islands of the sea. The inhabitants of Athos still believe this; and would it, indeed, be possible to find a peak whence the view, if not more vast, at least were more beautiful or more varied?

Outside the Hellenic world, where popular imagination was so poetical and so fertile, the people looked upon their mountains as the thrones of the lords of heaven and earth. Not only were the great summits of the Alps worshipped as the dwelling-place of the gods, and as the gods themselves, but even as far as the plains of Northern Germany and of Denmark, little hills, raising their brows above the uniform level, were Mounts Olympus, not less venerated than that of Thessaly had been by the Greeks; even in distant Iceland, in that land of fogs and eternal frosts, the worshippers of celestial sovereigns turned to the mountains of the interior, believing to behold in them the throne of their deities. Without doubt, had they been able to climb to the top of these volcanoes, furrowed with deep ravines, if they had beheld the horror of these craters wherein lava and snow incessantly struggled together, they would never have thought of making these terrible places the en-

chanted homes of their happy divinities. But they only
viewed these mountains from afar; they perceived the
peaks sparkling through the riven clouds, and pictured
them the more beautiful in proportion as the plains at
their base were wilder and more difficult to traverse.
These mountains, separated from the earth of mankind
by barriers of impassable precipices, were the city of
Asgard, where, beneath an ever-clement sky, dwelt the
blissful gods. The great cloud of vapors, ascending from
the summit of the divine mountain, and stretching far
athwart the sky, was no column of cinders; it was the
giant ash-tree Yggdrasil, beneath whose shadow reposed
the masters of the universe.

" THEY PERCEIVED THE PEAKS SPARKLING THROUGH THE RIVEN CLOUDS. "

Chapter XXI.

GENII.

RELIGIONS are slowly transformed. Those of the ancient world, apparently extinguished for so many generations, continue to exist beneath the exterior of modern beliefs. The names of the gods have frequently been changed, but the altar has remained the same. The attributes of the Divinity are still what they were two thousand years ago, and the faith which invokes it has preserved the "holy simplicity" of its fanaticism. In the wild valleys of Olympus, where gambolled the dishevelled Bacchantes, monks now mutter their prayers; upon holy Mount Athos, worshipped from the surface of the murmuring waves by mariners of every race and every tongue, nine hundred and thirty-six churches rise up in honor of all the saints; the God of Christians has become the heir of Zeus, who himself succeeded more ancient deities. Just so at Syracuse, the Temple of Minerva, whose golden spire the sailors saluted from afar by pouring a beaker of wine into the waters, has been changed into a church of the Holy Virgin. Every promontory running into the sea, and on land every brow of a hill, every mountain crowned with a temple, has retained its worshippers while changing its name. A traveller wanders over the Island of Cyprus in search of a temple of

Venus Aphrodite. "We no longer call her Aphrodite," devoutly cries the woman whom he questions; "we now call her the Chrysopolite Virgin."

But not only have Christian nations continued to venerate the sacred mountains of the Greeks and Romans, they have also propagated that religion in their own fashion throughout every country inhabited by them, in the same manner as our forefathers in legendary days. Our nearer ancestors, living in the Middle Ages, could not look upon a mountain without their imagination peopling its mysterious valleys and radiant summits with superior beings. It is true that these beings had no right to the title of gods: cursed by the Church, they transformed themselves into devils, into malevolent demons; or perhaps, tolerated by it, they became tutelary genii, unrecognized gods, merely invoked by stealth.

Jupiter, Apollo, Venus, having descended from their thrones, took refuge in the depths of caves; they whose august faces had beamed in light were condemned henceforth to live in the darkness of caverns.

The Olympic feasts were transformed into nocturnal revels, whither went hideous witches riding on brooms, to evoke the devil on tempestuous nights. Then, too, the cold climate, the cloudy sky of our northern countries, must have greatly contributed to the imprisonment of the ancient gods. How could they, beneath wind and snow, in the midst of storms, carry on their joyful banquets, enjoy their ambrosia, and play upon their golden lyres? We can hardly even in our dreams picture their presence in these fantastic palaces, constructed in one moment by the sun's rays upon those effulgent peaks, and vanishing not less quickly like visions or vain mirages!

Gods and genii **are the personification of all** that man dreads and desires. **All his terrors, all** his passions, formerly **assumed a supernatural form.** Some, too, among the mountain spirits **are** redoubtable magicians, who burn the grass **of the meadows, kill** the cattle, cast a spell over the passers-by; **others, on the** contrary, are benevolent beings, whose favor is conciliated by the libation of a bowl of milk, or even by a simple incantation. It is the good spirit that the shepherd implores to make his **lambs grow strong and his heifers** unblemished. **It is of him** especially **that young and old, male and female, ask that which unhappily would be for** almost all **the supreme** joy **of life—gold, riches, treasures.** Old traditions **tell us** how **the genii of the mountain glide into** the **veins of** the **stones** therein **to insert crystals and** metal, variously to mingle earth **and** minerals. Other **legends tell us** how **and** at what hour we must knock at **the** sacred **stone** hiding the riches; what signs **must** be **made, what** strange syllables **must be pronounced.** But let one item be forgotten, one sound **assume the** place **of another,** and all the formulas of incantation are futile.

I have seen enormous excavations undertaken **by** mountaineers at the **top of a rocky** point concealed **by snow during** nine months **in** the year. That point was consecrated to a saint, who himself had succeeded to a pagan deity as the guardian of the mountain. Each **summer the** treasure-seekers returned **to dig** farther into the summit, making use of sacramental **words and** gestures. **They** found nothing but **slabs of schist** beneath other **similar slabs;** yet, unwearyingly, some greedy digger would continue **his** work, striving to invoke the spirit by some **novel** formula, some victorious cry.

More interesting than these guardian deities of treasures are those who, in the mountain caverns, are charged
to preserve the genius of a whole race. Concealed in
the depths of the rock, they represent the entire people,
with its traditions, its history, its future. As old as the
mountain itself, they will endure as long as it; and so
long as they live will that race exist of which the various groups are scattered in the surrounding valleys. It
is the spirit who, in his profound thought, concentrates
all the bustle, all the flux and reflux, of the busy nation
at his feet. Thus the Basques look with pride at the
peak of Anie, where hides their god, unknown to the
priests, but all the more real. "So long as he is there,"
say they, "we shall be there too!" And willingly they
would believe themselves to be eternal, they whose language will disappear to-morrow!

To the same order of popular beliefs belong the legends of those warriors or prophets who, hidden in some
deep mountain cave, are awaiting the coming of the day.
Such is the myth of that German emperor who sat dream-
ing, leaning his elbows upon a table of stone, and whose
white beard, constantly growing longer, had taken root
in the rock. Sometimes a huntsman, perhaps a bandit,
would penetrate into the cavern and trouble the dream
of the mighty old man. The latter would slowly lift up
his head, ask a question of the trembling intruder, then
resume his interrupted dream. "Not yet!" sighed he.
For what was he waiting that he might die in peace?
No doubt the echo of some great battle, the odor of some
river of human blood, an immense revel in honor of his
reign. Ah! may that last battle have already been delivered, and the gloomy emperor now be nothing more
than a heap of ashes!

How much more touching, much more beautiful, is that
legend of the **three Switzers who are** also awaiting day-
break in the depths **of a lofty** mountain of the old **can-
tons!** They **are three, like those three who** in the **mead-**
ows of Grütli vowed to **set** themselves free; and all three
bear the name of Tell, as did **he who** overthrew **the ty-
rant.** They, too, sleep—they dream. **But it is** not of
glory that they are thinking; it **is** of liberty—not only
of Swiss liberty, but of that of all mankind. From time
to time one will go forth to look upon the world of lakes
and plains, yet sadly he returns to his companions. "Not
yet!" sighs he. **The** great day of deliverance is not come.
Ever slaves, the people have not ceased to worship their
masters' hats.

Chapter XXII.

MAN.

Let us wait, however, wait with confidence; the day will come; the gods will pass away, bearing with them the cortéges of kings, their melancholy representatives upon earth. Man is slowly learning to speak the language of liberty; he will also learn to practise its customs.

Those mountains which at least possess the merit of being beautiful belong to the number of gods whom we are beginning not to worship. Their thunders and avalanches have ceased to be for us the fulminations of Jupiter; their clouds are no longer the robe of Juno. Henceforth we can fearlessly invade the high valleys, the abode of the gods whither the genii repair. It is precisely the once-dreaded summits which have become the aim of thousands of travellers who have set before themselves the task of leaving not a single rock, not a single bed of ice, untrodden by human footsteps. In our populous countries of Western Europe every summit has already been successively conquered; those of Asia, Africa, America, will be so in their turn. Now that the era of great geographical discoveries is almost at an end, and, with the exception of a few lakes, the world is almost entirely known, other travellers, obliged to content themselves with lesser glory, dispute with one another, in great numbers the honor of being the first to ascend the as yet unvisited mountains. These climbing amateurs go as far as Greenland in search of some unknown summit.

Among them are some who, striving annually during the summer season to ascend a difficult lofty peak, are stirred by a vainglorious motive. People say that they seek a contemptible means of causing their names to be repeated in newspaper after newspaper, as if by a simple ascent they had performed some work of use to mankind. Arrived at the summit, with hands stiffened by the cold, they indite a detailed report of their triumph, noisily uncork bottles of champagne, fire off pistols like true conquerors, and frantically wave their flags. They bring several stones to that part of the mountain-peak which is not clothed with a dense cupola of snow, adding a few inches to its height. They are kings, lords of the world, since the whole mountain is to them but an enormous pedestal, and they behold kingdoms lying at their feet. They put out their hands as if to grasp it. It was thus that a rustic poet, invited for the first time to visit a royal castle, asked permission to ascend the throne for one moment. No sooner did he find himself there than the dizzy sensation of power took possession of him. He saw a fly flitting beside him. "Ah! I am a king now; I will crush you!" and with one blow of his doubled-up hand he stretched the poor insect upon the arm of the gilded chair.

Yet even the modest man—he who never talks of his ascents, and does not aspire to the ephemeral glory of having scaled some difficult peak—even he experiences great delight when he plants his foot upon a lofty summit. It was not merely with the wish of assisting science

that De Saussure kept his eyes fixed for years upon the
dome of Mont Blanc, that he made so many attempts
to ascend it. When, subsequently to Balmat, he did
reach the snow, until then inviolate, he was not only
delighted to be able to make fresh observations, but he
also indulged in the naïve happiness of having at last
surmounted that rebellious mountain. Both the huntsman who pursues animals and he who, alas! pursues man
are also delighted when, after a desperate chase through
woods and ravines, hills and valleys, they find themselves
face to face with their victim, and succeed in bringing
him down with a bullet. Fatigues, dangers, nothing has
stayed them, supported as they were by hope; and, now
that they rest beside their fallen prey, they forget all
that they have undergone. The mountain-climber, like
the huntsman, experiences the delight of conquest after
toil; yet he enjoys the pleasure all the more in that he
has risked none but his own life; he has kept his hands
unstained.

In making great ascents, danger is often very near,
and the risk of death run every moment; but on the
climber goes, feeling supported, kept up by a strong
sense of gladness at the contemplation of all those per-
ils which he knows how to avoid by the strength of his
muscles and his ready presence of mind. Frequently he
is obliged to creep along a slope of frozen snow, whereon
the slightest false step would dash him over a precipice.
At other times he crawls upon a glacier, hanging on to
a simple ledge of snow, which, if it were to give way,
would cast him into a fathomless gulf. Often, too, it
happens that he must scale walls of rocks by projections
hardly wide enough for one foot to find standing-room,

and which are covered with a crust of sheet-ice, **trem-bling, so to say,** under the influence of **the icy** water trickling beneath. But such are his courage and calmness of mind that **not a muscle allows** itself to make one wrong movement, and all is in perfect harmony in the effort to avert the danger. A traveller slips upon a steep rock of polished slate, ending abruptly at **the** edge of **a** precipice a hundred yards deep. He descends with dizzy rapidity down the slippery incline; but he stretches himself out at full length so as to **present a** larger **sur-face** of **friction and to take** advantage of every **little asperity of the rock; he uses his arms and legs so** skil-**fully as** brakes that at last he stops himself **on the edge of** the abyss. Just there a tiny streamlet ripples **over** the stone before tumbling down as a waterfall. **The traveller** was thirsty. He coolly drank, dipping his face in the water, ere he thought of getting up to resume his path over a less perilous rock.

The traveller **loves the mountain all the** more for the risk he runs of perishing upon it; but the sense of dan-ger overcome is not the only pleasure of the ascent, es-pecially to a man who during the course of his life-time has been obliged **to** undergo hard struggles in order to **do** his duty. **In** spite of himself, he cannot refuse **to** look upon the road just traversed, with its difficult passes, its snow, its crevasses, its obstacles of every kind, **as an** image of the toilsome path of virtue; this comparison of material matters with the moral world forces itself upon his mind. "In defiance of nature, **I** have succeeded," thinks he; "I have placed the summit beneath my feet; I have suffered, **it is true,** but I have conquered, and the task is accomplished." This feeling acts with all its

force upon those who make it a truly scientific mission
to ascend a dangerous height, either to study its rocks
and fossils, or to set up their instruments and sketch a
map of the country. They have, indeed, the right to
applaud themselves when they have gained the top; if
any evil befalls them on their journey, they have a right
to the dignity of a martyr. Grateful mankind ought to
remember their names, noble in a very different manner
from that of so many fictitiously great men!

Sooner or later the heroic ages of exploring mountains
must come to an end, as will that of exploring the earth
itself, and the fame of the renowned travellers will have
been transformed into a legend. One after another the
ascent of every mountain in populous countries will have
been made; easy footpaths, then driving-roads, will have
been constructed from the base to the summit, in order
to facilitate the means of access, even for those who are
worn out and feeble; a mine will have been sprung in
the crevasses of glaciers to show cockneys the texture of
the crystals; mechanical hoists will have been erected
upon the walls of mountains formerly inaccessible, and
" tourists " will allow themselves to be whisked up dizzy
heights while smoking their cigars and talking scandal.

But are we not already enabled to ascend mountains
by rail? Inventors have now produced hill locomotives,
so that we can plunge into the free air of the skies during the postprandial hour of digestion. Americans,
practical even in their poetry, have invented this novel
mode of ascent. In order, more quickly and without
fatigue, to reach the summit of their most venerated
mountain, to which they have given the name of Washington, the hero of their independence, they have con-

nected it with their railways. **Rocks and** pastures are encircled by a winding **iron road,** which the trains alternately ascend and descend, **whistling, and revolving their** wheels like **gigantic serpents. A** station is built upon **the summit, as** are refreshment-rooms and kiosks in the **Chinese** style. The traveller in search **of** ·views finds biscuits, liquor, and poems on the rising sun.

What the Americans have done for Washington the Swiss have hastened to copy for the Rigi, in the midst of that grandiose panorama of their lakes and mountains. They **have also** done **it for the Uetli, and will erelong do it for other** mountains; they **will, so** to say, bring **the summits** down to **the** level of the plains. Locomotives will pass from valley to valley away across the tops of mountains, **as a ship** rising and falling passes over the waves of the sea. As to such mountains as the loftiest peaks of the Andes and Himalayas, too high up **in the** regions of cold for man to go to their summits, the day will come, after all, **when he** shall be able to reach them. Balloons have already carried him two or three hundred thousand yards high; other aeronauts will bear and deposit him on Gaurisankar, as far as the "Great Diadem **of the** Dazzling Heaven."

In this great work of regulating nature, man does not confine himself to rendering mountains easy of **access;** **in** case of need, he labors to do away with them. Not contented with making driving-roads that ascend the most arduous mountains, engineers pierce the obstructing rocks, enabling their railways to pass through from valley to valley. **In spite** of all the obstacles placed across his path **by** nature, man moves on; he creates a new earth **adapted** to his wants. When he requires a

10

great harbor of refuge for his **vessels, he takes a cliff on** the sea-coast, and rock by rock casts it to the bottom of the ocean in order to construct a breakwater. Why, if the fancy seized him, should he not also take great mountains, triturate and scatter the remains upon the plains?

But stay! this work, too, has already been begun. **In** California the miners, weary of waiting until the streams should bring down the sand spangled with gold, have been inspired with the idea of attacking the mountain itself. In many places they crush the hard rock to extract the metal; but this work is difficult and expensive. The task is easier when they have a movable soil before them, such as shifting **sand and pebbles.** Then they **instal themselves before it, and** with enormous fire-pumps unceasingly wash down the sides with great jets of water, thus little by little demolishing the mountain to obtain every particle of gold it contains. In France they have thought of clearing away, in a similar manner, enormous heaps of ancient alluvions accumulated in plateaux in front of the Pyrenees; by means of canals, all this detritus, transformed into fertilizing mud, would serve to raise and cultivate the barren plains of the Landes.

These are, indeed, considerable steps of progress. The time is past when the only mountain roads **were such** narrow tracks that **two** pedestrians coming from contrary directions could not pass, and the one was obliged to walk across the back of **the** other lying upon the path. Every point of the earth will become accessible even to the sick and delicate; at the same time, every resource will be utilized, and man's life will thus find itself prolonged by every hour gained by his efforts, while **his** possessions are increased by all the treasures snatched from the earth. But, like everything human, this progress brings with it corresponding abuses; sometimes we should be on the **point** of cursing it, as formerly speech, writing, **books,** and even thought were cursed. Whatever **the lovers of** the good old times may say, life, so **rough for the** bulk of mankind, will yet become daily smoother. It is for us to see that a sound education shall arm the young man with an energetic will and render him ever capable of an heroic effort, the sole means of preserving mankind in its moral and natural vigor! **It** is for **us to replace** by methodical trials this hard battle of existence by which it is now necessary to purchase strength of mind. Formerly, when life was one incessant struggle between man and man or wild beasts, a youth was looked upon as a child until he had brought a bleeding trophy back to the paternal hut. He was obliged to prove the strength of his arm, the steadfastness of his courage, before he dared to lift up his voice in the council of **warriors.** In those countries where there was less danger of having to measure his valor with that of an enemy than of having to endure hunger, cold, and hardships, the candidate for **the** title of man would be left in a forest without food, without clothing, exposed to the biting wind and stinging insects; he was obliged to remain **there,** motionless, his face calm and proud, and after days of waiting he would, uttering never a complaint, still have determination enough to allow himself to be tortured, by assisting at an abundant repast without stretching out his hand to take his share. In these days such barbarous ordeals are not imposed upon our young people, but, at the risk of injuring and stupefying them, we must know how to arm our children with a lofty steadfast spirit, not only capable of resisting all possible evils, but especially all the temptations of life. Let us labor to render mankind happy, but let us at the same time teach it how to make its own happiness subservient to virtue.

In this excellent task, the bringing-up of our children, and through them of the future human species, the mountain has to play the principal part. Free nature with its beautiful landscapes, upon which we gaze, its laws, which we eagerly study from life, and its obstacles, too, which we must overcome, ought to be our real school. It is not in narrow rooms with barred windows that we can produce brave, true-hearted men. Let us rather grant them the delight of bathing in mountain lakes and torrents; let us take them out to wander over glaciers and fields of snow; let us lead them on to climb up lofty heights. Not alone will they thus learn without difficulty that which no book can teach them, not only will they remember all that they shall have learned in those blissful days when their impression of the professor's voice became blended with the view of lovely and vast scenery, but they will also find themselves confronted with danger, and they will have merrily faced it. Study will be a pleasure to them, and their character will be formed in gladness.

No one can doubt that we are on the eve of accomplishing most important changes in the aspect of nature as well as in the life of man. The external world, whose form we have already so powerfully modified, we shall, according to our custom, even still more vigorously transform. In proportion as our knowledge and material power increase, our will as men will manifest itself more and more imperiously towards nature. **At this very time** almost all so-called civilized nations still employ the greatest portion of their annual savings in preparing the means of killing one another and in mutually devastating their respective territories; but when, wiser, they shall apply themselves to augmenting the produce of the land, of jointly making use of all the powers of the earth, of doing away with all the natural obstacles raised by it against our free movements, then the whole appearance of the planet bearing us along in its vortex will be changed. Each nation **will, so to say, give a** new **vestment to the** nature surrounding it. By its fields, its **roads,** its dwellings, and its buildings of every kind, by the grouping of its trees and the general arrangement of **the** landscape, each nation will display the extent of its own taste. If it really possesses a sense of beauty, it will render nature more beautiful; if, on the contrary, the great mass of mankind should remain such as it is to-day, coarse, egotistical, and false, it will continue to imprint its sad qualities upon the world. Then would the poet's cry of despair become truth — "Whither shall I fly? Nature increases in hideousness!"

Whatsoever may be the future of man, or the aspect **of** the world which he may create for himself, solitude in that portion of nature which is left free will become more and more necessary to those men who wish to obtain renewed vigor of thought far from the conflict of opinions and voices. If the beautiful spots of the world should one day become a mere rendezvous for the worn and weary, those who **love** to live in **the** open air will have nothing left for them but to take refuge in a bark in the midst of the waves, or to wait patiently for the day when they shall be able to soar like a bird into the depths of space; but they would ever regret the fresh mountain valleys and the torrents bursting from un- trodden snow, and the white or rosy pyramids rising up in the blue vaults of heaven. Happily the mountains will always contain the sweetest places of retreat for him who flies from the beaten paths of fashion. For a long time yet we shall be able to turn aside from the frivolous world and find ourselves alone with our thoughts far from that flow of vulgar and factious opinions which dis- turbs and distracts even the most sincere minds.

What astonishment, what a breaking-off of all my habits, when, crossing the outlet of the last mountain de- file, I found myself once more in the vast plain, with its indistinct and fading background, its boundless space! The immense world was opened out before me; I could go to any point of the horizon whither fancy led me. And yet I seemed to be walking in vain; I could not get on, so completely had nature around me lost its charm and variety. No more could I hear the torrent, no more see the snow or rocks : it was ever the same monotonous landscape. My steps were free, and yet I felt that my imprisonment was very different from that of the moun- tain. One single tree, a mere shrub, sufficed to hide the horizon from me ; not a road which was not bounded on both sides by hedges or fences.

As I moved away from the beloved mountains rapidly receding from me, I often looked back to distinguish their fleeting forms. Gradually the slopes became con- fused in one uniform blue mass, the wide dips in the val- leys ceased to be visible, the lower peaks were lost to view, the contour of the higher summits alone stood out against the luminous background. At last the mist of dust and impurities rising from the plains hid the nethermost slopes of the mountains; nothing more remained save a sort of ornamentation bordering the clouds, and my eyes could hardly recognize any of the peaks I used to climb. Then all the outlines disappeared in vapor. The plain, void of all visible boundaries, surrounded me on every side. Henceforth the mountain would be far from me, and I had returned to the busy tumult of human beings. My memory has at least been able to preserve the sweet impressions of the past. Once more I see rising up before my eyes the beloved outlines of the mountains; mentally I re-enter the shady valleys, and for some moments I can enjoy in peace my intimate acquaintance with the rocks, the insects, and the blades of grass.

THE END.

RECLUS'S EARTH.

THE EARTH. A Descriptive History of the Phenomena of the Life of the Globe. By Élisée Reclus. Translated by the late B. B. Woodward, M.A., and Edited by Henry Woodward, British Museum. With 234 Maps and Illustrations, and 23 Page Maps printed in Colors. 8vo, Cloth, $5 00; Half Calf, $7 25.

Not only the vast amount of information concerning the phenomena of the physical world that is embodied in its contents, but the compactness and lucidity of its method, and the chaste beauty of its style, commend it to the attention of the intelligent reader, and promise equal delight and improvement from the diligent study of its pages. The writer treats, in the first place, of the Earth as a planet, comparing its dimensions with those of the sun and fixed stars, describing its motions and the succession of days and seasons, and discussing the various theories of its formation, and the duration of geological periods. The distribution of land and water is next considered, comprising a detailed account of continents, plains, deserts, mountains, glaciers, rivers, islands, lakes, and other prominent topics of physical geography, and concluding with the explanation of the subterranean forces which produce volcanoes, earthquakes, and great terrestrial upheavals and depressions. The chapters devoted to mountains and glaciers possess a fascinating interest, both on account of the clearness of their expositions and the picturesque grace of their natural sketches. The writer looks upon the wonders of the physical world with the eye and the heart of a genuine poet.—*N. Y. Tribune.*

For more than fifteen years this distinguished French *savant* travelled, explored, and studied the Earth, and the working of the elements which compose it. He has embodied the results of this travel and experience in a volume which, while satisfying the questions of an inquiring mind, does not tire. It is "exhaustive without being exhausting."—*Boston Traveller.*

Essentially popular in its character—that is, it is readable with pleasure by persons of ordinary intelligence, and a genuine attempt to popularize sound knowledge.—*Nation,* N. Y.

Published by HARPER & BROTHERS, New York.

☞ Harper & Brothers *will send the above work by mail, postage prepaid, to any part of the United States, on receipt of the price.*

RECLUS'S OCEAN.

THE OCEAN, ATMOSPHERE, AND LIFE. Being the Second Series of a Descriptive History of the Life of the Globe. By ÉLISÉE RECLUS. Translated from the French. Profusely Illustrated with 250 Maps or Figures, and 27 Maps printed in Colors. 8vo, Cloth, $6 00; Half Calf, $8 25.

Very many works have been written about the sea in its physical and emotional aspects, in its influence on the life of the planet, and its connection with mental development, but not one of them all is more remarkable than this, or contains a greater amount of information concerning "old Ocean's gray and melancholy waste."—*N. Y. Evening Post.*

For thorough research, rich attainments, and graphic style, M. Reclus holds high rank among the scientists of the day. It should be borne in mind that this work and its predecessor are written not for those already thoroughly versed in science, so much as for that much larger class of persons who seek to relieve the monotony of daily routine by the acquisition of some degree of knowledge, and who need books which, while accurate and in some sense profound, shall be free from technicalities and open to general understanding. Such books M. Reclus has furnished in these two volumes, which, taken jointly, cover a wide range of discussion. —*Boston Journal.*

It completes his descriptive history of the life of the globe, adding to the comprehensive description of the solid foundation, the bones, as it were, of the globe in the first volume, a like full statement of its circulating and life-giving media, the blood, of this greatest of animals, as some would have it. The first part, of two hundred pages, is a wonderfully thorough and philosophical, while popular, study of the ocean, its currents, tides, shallows, and shores; the second devotes as much more space to the atmosphere and meteorology; the third treats of animated life: the flora of the sea and earth, the fauna, "earth and man," and finally the work of man in his reaction on nature. The work is wonderfully comprehensive and informing, a very cyclopædia on its subject, interestingly readable in style, and in every respect of very great merit.—*N. Y. Evening Mail.*

PUBLISHED BY HARPER & BROTHERS, NEW YORK.

☞ HARPER & BROTHERS *will send the above work by mail, postage prepaid, to any part of the United States, on receipt of the price.*

FLAMMARION'S ATMOSPHERE.

THE ATMOSPHERE. Translated from the French of CAMILLE FLAMMARION. Edited by JAMES GLAISHER, F.R.S., Superintendent of the Magnetical and Meteorological Department of the Royal Observatory at Greenwich. With 10 Chromo-Lithographs, and 86 Woodcuts. 8vo, Cloth, $6 00; Half Calf, $8 25.

The style is very simple and comprehensive; there is an entire absence of puzzling technicalities, and everything necessary to be told is told in such a charming manner that even the most indifferent reader will find his interest excited, and his attention chained. We know of no other work on a similar subject which covers so wide a field. M. Flammarion apparently entered upon his task with an enthusiasm which shows no sign of flagging from the beginning to the end of the work. We do not know when we have found instruction and amusement more pleasingly combined than they are in this book, which is destined to enjoy a popularity second to none of the many works that have lately been issued with the laudable intention of popularizing science.—*Saturday Evening Gazette*, Boston.

This work is very comprehensive, treating of the form, dimensions, and movements of the earth, and of the influence exerted on meteorology by the physical conformation of the globe; of the figure, height, weight, color, and chemical components of the atmosphere; of the phenomena of light, heat, wind, clouds, rain, electricity; of the laws of climate, and, in short, of the wide range of subjects included under the general topic. It is very pleasing in style, and is profusely illustrated, ten full-page chromo-lithographs picturing the more remarkable phenomena mentioned.—*Boston Post.*

This is truly a superb volume, both externally and internally. As a piece of book-making, it marks the high degree of perfection to which the art is carried in the manufactories of the publishers. The literary side of the work is creditable alike to the French author and the English editor, who here bring their several national traits into a happily combined co-operation.—*Christian Advocate*, N. Y.

PUBLISHED BY HARPER & BROTHERS, NEW YORK.

☞ HARPER & BROTHERS *will send the above work by mail, postage prepaid, to any part of the United States, on receipt of the price.*